Rainbow Spies 3
La Conclusione Italiana

By

William Green

Table of Contents

Table of Contents

Continued

Prologue

The North Italian Mafia, the Nuevo Mala Del Brenta, is selling arms to ISIS in Syria in exchange for heroin. The American Mafia is selling arms to the Italian Mafia in exchange for heroin. The arms are stolen from American arms manufactures. With very little capital investment by the American Mafia, the flow of arms for heroin is pure profit for both the American and Italian Mafia.

CIA agents Peg O'Ryan and Marc Parker are assigned under cover in the Northern Italian Mafia. They both become paramours of male members of the Family. Marc is gay. Their assignment is to disrupt the flow of arms and heroin or in the best case, destroy the flow.

Chapter 1

CIA Headquarters

Langley, Virginia

Present Day Early Morning

Ring

"Hello."

"Hi Marc, it's Peg. Peter wants to see us in his study. He's got a new assignment for us."

"Did he say what it was?"

"Nope. He said that he didn't want to discuss it over the phone."

"Okay, I'll swing by your office and we can go together."

For whatever reason, Marc's office was in another wing of the building. Because they worked almost exclusively with each other, Marc and Peg have tried, without success, to relocated near each other. Five minutes later, Marc stuck his head in Peg's door.

Hi, Peg O'my heart, ready to go?"

"Sure." Peg followed Marc out the door. They walked for another five minutes before they reached their supervisor Peter's office in another building.

Peter's secretary, Virginia looked up as they entered. "He's expecting you. Go on in."

Marc knocked and in response to a muffled "Enter", held the door open for Peg and followed her into the room.

"Hi Peter, you wanted to see us?" Marc asked.

"Yes," Peter responded. "Shut the door and seat yourselves. I have an assignment for your that I believe is well suited to you two. How's your Italian?"

Both Peg and Marc answered "Bene."

"Good. Because you are going under cover with the Northern Italian Mafia."

"We've gotten intel that the American and Italian Mafia are shipping arms to ISIS in Syria. What we know so far, is that arms are being stolen here in the United States. Then they are making their way through the Italian Mafia to ISIS in exchange for heroin. The heroine coming into the United States by way of the American Mafia for the American drug trade."

"The National Security Agency, the Federal Bureau of Investigation and the Arms, Tobacco, Alcohol and Explosives agency (ATF) have put together a team to handle operations here in the United States. They came to us to take the lead in foreign affairs. We also have a liaison with the Italian Agency for External Information and Security; the AISE. Any questions so far?"

Peg and Marc looked at each other and Marc gave a nod to Peg. "If we're going under cover in the Mafia, aren't we going to stand out? The Mafia are probably swarthy. With my red hair and green eyes and Marc's blue eyes, it seems we'd stand out and not in a safe way."

"That's where the AISE comes in. You will be Northern Italians descendent belonging to the America Mafia Family; the Nuova Mala Del Brenta or Mafia Veneta. Giovanni De Luca, a high-level Mafia boss, is currently behind bars and is willing to give you introduction to his Family. They supposedly want in on the heroin traffic, so they can distribute it in Europe."

"How's that supposed to work?" asked Marc.

"De Luca is still very powerful. He runs the Mafia inside the prison and outside as well. So, with a reduced sentence and some perks within the prison, he's willing to make the introductions."

"And we're supposed to trust him?" Peg asked.

"Only to a point." Peter responded. "He believes you are American Mafia and are going to get him a slice of the heroin trade for his assistance in the flow of arms to Syria. As part of your cover, you are both lieutenants and are authorized to negotiate with the Nuova Mala Del Brenta. Any more questions?"

Peg and Marc looked at each other and then shook their heads.

"Okay, let's go to the conference room and you can meet the rest of the team."

The trio walked a few yards and entered the conference room. A large room with frosted glass walls an oblong mahogany table and twelve leather chairs. Seated inside were seven men and one woman. They rose as they entered.

"Gentlemen and lady," Peter began, "these are my agents Margret O'Ryan and Marcus Parker. Peg, Marc On the right are FBI agents Steve Lerner and his partner Max Honer. Next to them are NSA agents Luke Steve and his partner Lois Gable and to the left are ATF agents Sam Bear and Clark Newson."

Peg and Marc shook their hands as they were introduced.

Two Men stood off from the group. Peter nodded his head at them. "These two gentlemen are our liaison to the Italian government, AISE agents, Alfredo Beloni and Dominico Cervelli."

Both men dipped their heads but did not offer a hand shake.

"Everyone please, take a seat," Peter said. With the help of the AISE," Peter nodded to Beloni and Cervelli, "Peg and Marc will go under cover in the Nuova Mala Del Brenta."

"The ATF is taking the lead on operations here in the States, supported by the FBI and NSA." Motioning with his hand at the two ATF agents, "Would one of you give us an overview on arms manufacturing and traffic here in the States?"

"Sure," Bear spoke up. "Making weapons has become a U.S. specialty, with 47 American companies filling the top 100 grossing slots in the world. They are selling about $235 Billion a year to the Armed Services. Some of the weapons make their way overseas to support American operation and, our allies. By far the rest are stored in military depots or at any given time, about 30% are in transit to those depots."

"Here's where a major problem occurs. The transporters are the manufactures, and unlike military transporting, they don't have an armed escort, making them targets for hijacking. Most of the depots are in rural areas with little or no other road traffic. So, they block the road, pull the driver out at gun point, drive the rig to another location, transfer the cargo, and vanish."

"Do you have any idea where the arms go from there?" Marc asked.

"Not really. Our best guess is the arms go to New Jersey immediately after the hijacking, are loaded on a cargo vessel, hidden under legitimate cargo and make their way to Venice, Italy. This is based on sightings that, unlike the manufacture's trucks, they have a Mafia armed escort. They ae easy to spot. The Mafia aren't the only ones interested in getting their hands-on military weapons."

"Can't you stop them?" Peg asked.

"No. Their trucks are unmarked, so we can't get a search warrant."

"What happens after Venice?" Peg spoke again.

"We've no idea. That's where the two of you come in. Once you've joined the Nuova Mala Del Brenta, the rest of the route to Syria, is for you to learn."

Peter asked if either the FBI or NSA had anything to add. They shook their heads in unison. As the group stood, and began to file out of the room, Peter asked the two Italian agents to stay.

The two men moved back to the table and sat opposite Marc and Peg.

"Can you give Marc and Peg a rundown on their contact for the Nuova Mala Del Brenta."

"Si Signore. Mi scusi." Beloni spoke. "I mean yes sir."

Peter spoke. "I don't speak Italian, but if you are more comfortable speaking in your native tongue, Marc and Peg both speak Italian."

"No, that's good. We both need to practice our English." Cervelli replied with only a slight accent.

"your English is quite good." Peg remarked. "Will you give us the information we need to get integrated in the Nuova Mala Del Brenta Family?"

"One of their lieutenants will meet you at the Aeroporto di Venezia. They will have pictures of you, so they will find you. They will have a car waiting and will take you to a villa in the Friuli-Venezia Giulia area Northeast of Veneta. There you will meet Don Giovanni's second-in-command Luigi Visconti. From there on, you are on your own."

"How does that work? Asked Marc.

"They will think they are getting a visit from the American Mafia." Beloni replied.

"How about communications?" Marc asked again.

"You will keep your current cell phones, assuming they are secure, so you can keep in touch with Peter and we will give you two more secure cell phones so, you can contact us. We'd like to setup a schedule for updates, say, 11:00 PM, but they may not always be possible. We will not call unless it's an emergency. Our caller ID will show an American exchange."

"We won't be using our real names, so I will be Pietro Romano and Peg will be Magdalena Rossa."

Cervelli snickered. "Did you know Rossa means red as in red hair?"

Peg laughed. "No, so I guess I'll be changing it. How about Conti?"

"That will work." Cervelli replied.

Marc chuckled. "So that will be the names on our passports. We should be able to leave in two days. After we've made the air reservations, we'll get you the information so, you can pass it on to whomever is meeting us. When are you are going home?"

"We leave tomorrow morning." Belone answered.

"Okay. I'll make the flight arrangements this afternoon and get the information to you." Peg responded. "Peter, I assume you have their contact info?"

Peter nodded and stood. "Gentlemen, thank you for your assistance." Leaning across the table to shake their hands.

Peg and Marcus followed suit.

Marcus Parker and Margaret O'Ryan were a CIA covert team. They had been working cases together for about five years and had developed complimentary techniques. Their personal relationship had also blossomed. It would never go beyond brother-sister feelings though; Marc is gay.

Peg was striking with her red hair, green eyes and a spray of freckles across the bridge of her nose, leaving little doubt of her Irish ancestry. She was tall, five eight, with a runner's body. Running and practicing her martial arts skills were two things she enjoyed most.

Marc was six-one, muscular, with dark hair and blue eyes. His skin had an olive tone that he hoped to darken while they were in sunny southern California. Appearing as a couple was one of their cultivated personas. They seemed to be focused on each other but in truth, they were scanning the people moving around them. Their training made them constantly aware of their surroundings. Marc and Peg also had an ongoing game of guessing the sexual leanings of the men they came across.

Both Marc and Peg were students of Shaolin Chin Na martial arts style. They originally sparred together, but realizing their moves were becoming easy to read, they eventually sought out other agents to broaden their skills.

Chapter 2

CIA Headquarters

Langley, Virginia

Present Day Noon

Peter left for his office while Peg and Marc headed for their offices in the other buildings.

"It looks as if we are going to have some excitement." Peg commented.

"Yeah, finally. These last two months have been really boring." Marc responded.

"Did you see the way Alfredo Beloni was staring at me?" Marc asked.

"I sure did. I don't think he took his eyes off you for the whole meeting and you stared back."

"Yeah, I did, and he winked at me. He's nice looking, but I'd only be interested in a one-night stand. He's leaving in the morning so that's out. Maybe I'll see him in Italy once this case is over."

"Let's go to my office and I'll call Travel to get us setup." Peg said.

The five-minute walk was made in silence, as each generating scenarios for their new characters. They entered Peg's office — she going to her desk and Marc flopping in the guest chair. As Peg picked up her phone, Marc opened his laptop to research the Nuova Mala Del Brenta Family. Twenty minutes later, she disconnected and finished scribbling a few notes.

"We're booked on British Airways for day after tomorrow for a red-eye that stops over at Heathrow Airport and then on to Venice. We leave at 6 PM. It gets into Venice airport about noon of the following day."

Marc groaned. "I hate Heathrow. Every time you turn-around you're going through another security check."

'I'm with you on that, but that was the best Travel could do." Peg said. "At least, we're in business class, so we should be able to sleep."

"I dug up some background information on Nuova Mala Del Brenta." Marc said. "Listen to this. This Family started up in the 1970s by Felice Maniero. There was a bunch of Sicilian Mafia members imprisoned in the Venice area to keep them isolated from main Family in Sicily. There were several, loosely organized local gangs, operating in Venice and the surrounding area with the backing of the Sicilian Mafia."

"Maniero pulled together the Clan Giostrai, the Mestrini group, the Veneziani, the old crime underworld of Venice, and the San Don di Piave cartel into what was known then as the Mala Del Brenta. There were, at that time, 400 – 500 members. Their activities spanned about every criminal activity known."

"Maniero was captured in 1993. He turned informant which resulted in the arrest of more than 400 Mafia members. Officials considered the Mala Del Brenta to be finished."

"In 1996, the remnants of the gang staged a robbery at the Mirabilandia theme park that netted them 350 billion Lira ($214,000). This launched the Nuova Mala Del Brenta Mafia."

"Wow," Peg remarked. "That's quite a history. Of all the Latin races, the Italians are the most family oriented in the traditional sense and in the Mafia."

"Let's head down to see the Wizard and see what he may have

 for us."

The "Wizard", the nickname for Mike Simmons, was a scientist extraordinaire. He designed and produced equipment for field agents.

Peg and Marc took the elevator to the fourth sub-basement. They exited the elevator directly into Mike Simmons large laboratory. There were several people working at computers and others who were seated or standing next to stainless steel table working on various "gadgets". They walked up to a tall thin man who stood with his back to them.

"Mike," Peg said.

The man stopped his task and turned. "Peg, Marc, how are you?" Before they could answer, he said: "You are going on an assignment and need some of my special toys – right?"

"You got me in one." Peg responded. "We're going under-cover into the Italian Mafia and wanted to see what you have that could make our job easier."

"Let's see. I have watches that will record voice and send it to your cell phones. I have eye glasses that will record voice and what you're seeing and send it to your cell phones. The data from either the watches or eye glasses can be stored on your phones or transmitted back to Langley real-time. There is an added feature, press the left stud on the watch and a curved blade will deploy. I've got metal pencils and pens what will work as they are designed to look, but will spit a small dart that will incapacitate the average person for about sixty minutes. Range is about ten feet. And, I can provide pistols that are common to the American Mafia, so you can leave your CIA issued weapons here."

"That's quite a menu," Marc said. "I think I should take the glasses, we both should have the watches, and I think we both should have the pens. Is that okay with you, Peg?"

"Sure, I'm fine with that." She said

"Okay," Mike responded. "I can have everything ready about 10 in the morning. Can you leave your cell phones with me for about an hour? I need to load some application software on them, then checkout links between the devices, to your phones and the link to Langley."

"Sounds good," Marc replied.

They both handed over their phones and shook Mike's hand and headed back to the elevator.

"I want to check on the weather in North Italy, so we'll know what to pack. How are we going to explain having weapons in our luggage when we get to the villa?"

"If it comes up, we'll just say, we have a friend in the TSA at the airport, who sees that our luggage doesn't go through x-ray. For a small gratuity of course. The same goes for Heathrow."

They stood in the hallway beside the elevators. "I need to get some of my cases reassigned." Peg said.

"Likewise," Marc responded. "I'll meet you in Mike's lab at ten tomorrow morning. Okay?"

Peg nodded, and they went to their respective offices.

<h1 style="text-align:center">Chapter 3</h1>

<h2 style="text-align:center">Dulles Airport, Virginia</h2>

Marc's phone rang. Caller ID showed Peg. "Hi Peg, what's up? From now on, I'll should be calling you Magdalena or Maggi, If that's okay."

They had traveled separately to the airport.

"Maggi is good. I just arrived, Pietro. Where are you?"

"I'm at the ticket counter checking in. I'll wait for you here."

Marc had not finished checking in before Peg was waiting two people back in the check-in line.

After Peg caught up to Marc, they headed to the British Airways lounge. Each settled in well-padded lounge chairs and opened their lap tops.

"I want to get more information on the second-in-command, Luigi Visconti." Marc studied his computer for a while. "Doesn't seem to be much information on him. He's thirty-five. That's young for his position. Says he's unmarried — no children. Doesn't mention any current girlfriend. He's nice looking." Marc turned his computer, so Peg could see.

"Looks like your type," Peg commented.

"Right. I wouldn't turn him down. Like they say: keep your friends close and your enemies closer. Might be a plan."

"Couldn't get much closer than in bed with him," Peg said. "I could almost bet, when the head honcho is locked away for life, the subs will be maneuvering for ways to climb to the top. You'll need to be careful you don't get pulled into some conspiracies."

"Yeah, but if I could get close to him, we'd probably learn how the pipe-line works for getting the weapons to Syria and the drugs back to Italy and the United States. Anyway, this is a lot of supposition. We'll just have to see how thing plays out."

"We should probably get to our gate. They should be boarding soon," Peg said.

They arrived at the gate just as Business Class was boarding. They quickly found their seats and buckled-in.

"They will most likely serve dinner right away and I plan on sleeping right after that. It's a little over seven hours to Heathrow and then a couple more to Venice.

Fortunately, these seats recline all the way flat, so we should get five to six hours sleep." Peg remarked.

Dinner was served just after the plane reached cruising altitude. The meal was light, and they passed on alcohol as red-eyes and booze didn't mix.

Their last words were:

"'Night, Maggi."

"'Night, Pietro."

Chapter 4

Marco Polo Airport

Venice Italy

After they exited the secure part of the air terminal, they saw several people holding signs with arriving passenger's names.

"Look," Peg said. "That looks like our ride."

A young, dark headed man dressed in an expensive suit was holding a paper sign with the names: Conti and Romano in bold letters. They walked up to him.

"Signore Romano, Signorina Conti sarò il tuo autista. Mi chiamo. Al tuo servizio." " Mister Romano, Miss Conti I will be your driver. My name is Alfredo. At your service."

"Grazie Alfredo. Lei parla inglese?" Do you speak English?"

"Yes, I do," Alfredo responded with only a slight accent. "But your Italian is excellent."

"I'm working on it, but we don't speak much Italian at home so I'm a little rusty." Marc answered.

"Come this way to get your luggage and we'll soon be on our way to the Villa."

They pointed out their luggage to Alfredo. He would not allow them to carry their own. Staggering under two large and two small bags, Alfredo led them to a black limousine parked at the curb.

Marc noted the no-parking signs. Even though there was a policeman standing near, the limo wasn't ticketed. *"Must be nice,"* he thought.

They loaded into the limo. As they pulled away from the curb, Marc asked, "Alfredo, how far to the villa?"

"Sixty kilometers or about an hour, Signore."

Marc and Peg were mostly silent on the ride, except for answering a continual stream of questions, from Alfredo, about New York.

They turned off the highway onto a gravel road for about half mile through olive groves. The villa had pale yellow stucco, red tile roof and iron railing on the balconies.

Pulling up to the villa, Marc remarked: "Looks more like a fortress than a villa. Look at the security." There were armed guards patrolling the grounds and more posted on the many balconies.

"Si, we are very secure," Alfredo added. "Come inside and I will introduce you to Signore Visconti. Your luggage will be sent to your rooms."

Above the entrance was engraved a raptor and below the words: Villa del Falco.

Chapter 5

Villa del Falco

Friuli-Venezia Giulia, *Italy*

Alfredo led them up the marble stairs and through a large wooden entry door, held open by another guard. The foyer was two stories high. The floors were also marble. A wide staircase more marble, wound in a graceful curve up to the next floor.

"This way, Signorina, Signore." Alfredo led them to double sliding wood doors and opened one side. He ushered them in and closed door, remaining outside. Standing by the fireplace, was large muscular man with black hair. His features were handsome.

"More so than his picture," Marc thought.

The man moved toward them hand extended. "Signorina, Signore benvenuto. Miss, Mister welcome. Sono il tuo ospite Luigi Visconti. I am your host Luigi Visconti." He took Peg's hand first. "Signorina Conti?" He released her hand.

"Si," Peg answered. "Piacere di conoscerti." "I am pleased to meet you."

Visconti turned and took Marc's hand. "Signore Romano?"

"Si," Marc repeated. "Piacere di conoscerti.

Visconti held Marc's for several seconds as he stared into his eyes. "Per favore, chiamami Luigi." "Please call me Luigi." Visconti smiled.

Marc returned his smile. "Chiamami Pieto."

Visconti responded in English. "Your accents are little heavy. Would you prefer we speak in your native tongue?"

"Thank you, Luigi. We don't usually speak Italian at home. Just when we are talking to our grandparents."

"Come." Luigi led them to French doors that

opened to a large patio. "Lunch is ready."

The patio was ringed with stone balustrades — the view was slopping fields, olive groves and woodlands leading up to a large sculptured garden.

"This is beautiful," Peg said. "Do you own all this land?"

"No," Luigi responded. Everything here is owned by Don Giovanni De Luca. I just hold it in trust for him.

"But we were told he has a life sentence," Peg said.

"Makes no difference," Luigi responded. Either inside or outside, he is still the Don."

"And, when he dies, do you inherit?" Marc asked.

"Not necessarily," Luigi answered. "He has appointed me second-in-command, but if he passes, there will be a power struggle. The strongest will take over."

"Are you prepared for this?" Marc asked.

"Yes. I would be the youngest Don ever, but I have a lot of respect from the other lieutenants."

Luigi directed them to a square pavilion centered on the patio. The patio over looked an Olympic size pool. The table was set with fine china, crystal goblets and silverware. Two men, who appeared to be servants, waited with hands clasp.

"Please sit down." Luigi held a chair for Peg. "We will be having lobster bisque with a Pinot Grigio, and then we will have roast duck paired with a nice Chianti. Is this to your satisfaction?"

Both Peg and Marc nodded. Luigi motion to the two men and they went to the house. Shortly, they returned with a large tureen, which they placed on a side table. One man took the soup bowls from the table to the side table where the second man ladled the bisque into each. One man served Peg's soup first, then the two servants served Marc and Luigi.

Conversation was light — touching on the weather, New York and things to see and do in Northern Italy. Marc was puzzled that Luigi did not bring up the purpose of their visit. He later learned that at the Villa, business was never discussed during meals. When they had finished with a desert of fruit and coffee, Luigi suggested that they move to his office.

Luigi unlocked a large wooden door and pushed it open. He motioned Peg and Marc into the room and had them sit themselves in two burgundy leather chairs facing his desk. The room had dark wooden floors, dark wood paneling and leaded glass windows. Luigi seated himself and asked: "Would you like to smoke?" Both Peg and Marc in unison said: "I don't smoke.".

"Va bene." Luigi responded. Opening a humidor, he pulled out a cigar. "Do you mind if I smoke?"

"No problem," Marc answered.

Luigi lighted his cigar and leaned back in his chair. "Shall we talk business now?" Marc nodded his acceptance. "What is it that you hope to accomplish here?"

Peg and Marc looked at each other and Peg motioned her hand to Marc. "We have been instructed to observe your operation in detail to see if it would be feasible to increase the supply of arms to your organization. If so, it would be most beneficial to both of our organizations. We are interested to see if your pipeline can handle an increase and how much of an increase it could tolerate. Currently, we are dividing the heroin on a thirty-seventy percent split. We are authorized to increase your take, if this can be accomplished."

"How much of an arms flow increase are we talking about?" Luigi asked.

Marc looked at Peg again and Peg nodded. "We need to go through the whole process. Then we will be able to see how much more you can handle."

"I'm sure we can accommodate you. Where would you like to start?" Luigi replied.

Peg spoke up. "We are familiar with the first leg as we have looked at the operation in New Jersey, and we both believe that, the ships you're using, can handle an increase. What we'd like to see how the second leg works. We understand that a similar ship is used to transport the arms from here. In particular, we want to understand how the land transfer is accomplished in Syria."

"Let me show you a map." Luigi pulled open a drawer and took out a rolled paper. Mark took out his glasses and put them on.

Luigi spread the map on his desk. "Here is the west coast of Syria. We dock at the port of Latakia where we transfer the arms to trucks supplied by ISIS. Then we take this route." Luigi trace his finger south from Latakia alone highway M1, then inland to Homs.

"You are responsible for the arms until they reach Homs?" Asked Marc. "Why is that?"

"Yes," Luigi responded. "ISIS is under siege in Homs and they claim, using their people, would weaken their defenses."

"One other question," Peg added. "why not use the same ship that comes from New Jersey to go on to Latakia? It seems a waste of man power and extra costs."

"It's a ship registry problem. The ship from New Jersey is registered in the United States and the port authority at Latakia will only allow ship from other Muslin countries. In this case Lebanon."

"We can accommodate you on this next part of the process. You must be aware, that the land trip in Syria is very dangerous. We often are besieged by other rebel groups trying to hijack our shipments." Luigi said.

"Marc and I can handle ourselves. We both are armed, and we are assuming that you can supply us with automatic weapons for the land trip."

"But of course," Luigi responded. "Now, it's our custom to have a period of rest in the afternoon for a few hours. I'm sure you both would like to refresh yourselves after your long plane trip." Luigi pushed a button on his desk and the door, behind them, opened and a man entered. "This is Carlo. He will show you to your rooms and come to get you later this afternoon. We will meet in the great room for cocktails. In Italy, we usually dine at nine, but in deference to your American custom, we will eat earlier tonight, but for this night only." He smiled and came around the desk to shake their hands.

Luigi shook Peg's hand first. She noticed that he held Marc's hand longer while looking intently into his eyes. *Looks like Marc has made a conquest.* Peg thought.

They followed Carlo up the stair and down a wide hallway. "Signorina, questa sarà la tua stanza." "Miss this will be your room." Carlo said. The door opened to a large room with a canopied bed, polished floor and Persian rugs.

"Very nice," Peg muttered.

Marc followed Carlo to the next door and opened it to a similar room.

"Signore." Carlo motioned with his hand.

"Grazie." Marc responded. He entered the room and listened at the door until he could no longer hear Carlo's footsteps. Opening the door, he looked both ways down the hall. Moving to Peg's door, he knocked softly.

Peg immediately open her door as if she had been anticipating Marc's arrival. Marc put his finger to his lips and motioned that they should go out onto the balcony.

Marc spoke softly. "I don't want to take the chance they had the room bugged. Looks like we're in. Getting a picture of the map was a stroke of luck. If this is the route, the arms convoy always takes, I have an idea how to put a kink in their supply line."

"What do you have in mind," Peg asked

"Simple. Assuming we can get a timetable, we can call in an air strike. They would probably put it down to a random hit on a rebel supply line by the Syrian air force."

They both returned to their rooms for a nap.

At 5 PM, there was a gentle knock on each of Peg and Marc's door. Carlo escorted them to the great-room where Luigi was seated.

"Ah, you both look more refreshed." Luigi remarked.

"Thank you, Luigi, that was a welcome respite." Marc responded. "The rooms are very nice."

"Yes, they are." Peg echoed.

Luigi motioned to a bar in the corner of the room. "What will you have to drink?"

"I'd like a gin and tonic please." Peg said.

Luigi turned to Marc with a questioning gaze.

Marc responded with: "Scotch for me—neat no ice please."

"A man after my own heart. Luigi said moving to the bar. We have Bombay Safire gin for the lady and Dalmore King Alexander III single malt scotch for the gentleman."

"Bombay's my standard." Peg remarked.

"Dalmore exceeds my standard," Marc said. You are more than a man after my own heart."

Luigi smiled and Marc and winked. "I certainly hope so."

Marc returned his smile with a nod of his head.

Peg thought to herself. *"Not surprised."*

Luigi motioned them to a sitting area by a massive fireplace. He poured their drinks and carried them over to where they were seated.

Again, their upcoming business was not discussed. Luigi told them that he had never been to New York, so the conversation revolved around that city. He never asked about their "Family" activities. He seemed to be fascinated about the night life and cultural events. Peg's and Marc's drinks were refreshed two more times as they talked for the next two hours. Carlo appeared at the door and announced that dinner was ready.

Luigi stood and said: "This way please." Motioning with his hand. He directed them across the hall to the dining room. Again, the table was set with fine china, silverware and crystal. The room was paneled with the same dark wood. Ringed around the room were portraits of stern looking men. Luigi waved his hand at the portraits and remarked: "Former great men of our Family."

Three places were set and on the end of a large table. Luigi stood behind the chair to the left and pulled it out for Peg. He motioned to Marc to take a seat opposite Peg and then took his place at the head of the table.

Luigi nodded to Carlo. He took plates of fresh slice tomatoes topped with mozzarella cheese and basil from the side-board and placed them in front of each diner.

Conversation was light as they progressed to servings of a white fish. The next course was Pappardelle with Cinghaile.

"Ah, remarked Marc. Wild boar. My favorite."

"I'm pleased," Luigi said. "you are true to your Italian roots."

The dinner was finished with chocolate gelato topped with a chocolate-cherry sauce. They returned to the great-room and Carlo served them snifters of Armagnac. Luigi again offered a cigar to Marc, which he refused. He lighted one for himself.

The conversation returned to New York and other major cities in the United States. An hour later, Peg asked to be excused claiming jet lag. Luigi and Marc stood as she left the room.

"How about you Marc," Luigi asked. "Do you need to retire?"

"Not right now." He replied. "I'm good for a while, if that's okay with you."

"More than okay. I'd like to get to know you better." Luigi stared directly into Marc's eyes. "Can I ask you a personal question?"

"Certainly." Marc responded.

"Are you gay?" Luigi noted that Marc did not seem to be startled or uncomfortable with the question.

"Yes, I am." He replied. "Is that a problem?"

"No—not at all. I myself am bisexual and I find myself attracted to you."

Marc let a smile cross his face. "And, I find myself attracted to you."

Luigi stood and offered a hand to Marc. "Shall we continue this discussion upstairs?"

Marc smiled again. "Certainly."

Luigi led Marc to another room on the same floor as their rooms. He opened a door and ushered Marc through. The room was larger the ones Peg and Marc occupied but appointed in much the same.

"Very nice," Marc said.

Luigi closed the door and came up behind Marc. He wrapped his arms around Marc and leaned into his neck; breathing in his scent. Marc turned to face him and lowered his hands to Luigi's waist. They were about the same height; Luige brushed his lips across Marc's. Marc drew back a little, enjoying the taste of Armagnac and tobacco. He stared into Luigi's eyes for a moment, then pulled Luigi into a deeper kiss.

They both worked at each other's clothing until they were naked. Each of their members were extended as if they were preparing for a duel. They moved into another passionate embrace; Luigi took Marc's hand and led him to the bed.

Next morning, Marc knocked on Peg's door. She responded with "Give me a few minutes."

Marc answered: "I'll be down stair looking for coffee. Catch up with me there."

A muffled "Okay" came through the door.

Marc came into the dining room and found Luigi with a cup of coffee reading the newspaper. "Good morning Luigi. Did you sleep well?"

"Yes, I did." He replied. "Especially after a wonderful evening. Thank you."

"Yes, it was special, wasn't it?" Marc smiled. He leaned forward and brushed lips crossed Luigi's.

At that point, Peg entered the room. "Am I interrupting,' she asked.

Marc chuckled.   "Not at all, Maggi. Can I pour you some coffee?" He said as he moved to the sideboard.

"Please," she responded. "After all that food and drink last night and jet lag, I need a large cup."

Carlo appeared at the door and asked if he could serve breakfast. Luigi nodded, and he returned with platters of eggs, bacon and sweet Italian sausage and placed them on the sideboard. He added plates, silverware, napkins, goblets and a large pitcher of orange juice.

Luigi stood and motioned to Peg and Marc. "Please help yourselves."

After serving themselves, Marc asked: "What's the plan for today?"

Luigi held up a hand to stop Marc. "After we eat."

The conversation was light again. Peg was interested in the land surrounding the villa. Luigi said that the property extended about 10 kilometers around the villa. He added that most of the land was sublet to farmers. The gardens around the villa were maintained by a dedicated crew. He said that there were twenty guards both day and night - armed.

Marc asked: "I noticed the word Falco above the lintel when we first arrived. That means Falcon doesn't it?"

"Yes," Luigi replied. "One of the out buildings is a falconry where I train falcons. It's one of my hobbies or I should say one of my passions. Would you be interested in seeing it and perhaps going on a hunt?"

Both Peg and Marc replied enthusiastically," Yes, that would be great." They laughed at having spoken the same words simultaneously.

Luigi finished his coffee and stood. "There will be a car at the front in an hour to take us to the harbor. A ship arrived this morning from the States. You can observe the transfer of the guns and ammunition to the next vessel for the trip to Syria. Until then, will you please excuse me? I need to make some phone calls."

"Certainly," Peg responded. "Marc and I need to talk."

Luigi left the room and Peg turned to Marc. "Let's go out to the patio. It's such a beautiful day, I want to enjoy it while we can." Peg winked at Marc.

Later outside, putting her index finger to her lips, Peg said: "let's go into the garden." They didn't speak until they were on the far side of the swimming pool. "Okay," she said. "Report."

"what do you mean report?"

"I mean, I heard you go to your room around midnight. So, what happened?"

"Well, Luigi and I connected last night." Marc explained.

"You mean, he's gay?"

"Not exactly," he responded. "He says, he's bi-sexual, but that the default code for gay Italian men. He's what, thirty-five and never married. My money's on gay not bisexual."

"Okay, I'm glad you got some action but why you and not me?"

"your turn will come." Marc laughed.

"We'll see," Peg responded. "What's our next move?"

"We need to be critical of his operation and look for a chance to suggest, strongly, that he expand."

They talked of different options until it was time to meet Luigi at the car.

Chapter 6

Molo Audace

Friuli-Venezia Giulia, Italy

The car waiting for them was a black BMW limo. Both the driver and the man in the passenger seat were dressed in black suits. They appeared to be more of Luigi's security team.

Luigi held the door open and motioned Peg and Marc in. Once he was seated, he directed the driver. "Molo Audace and take the coast route."

Marc spoke: "I'm not familiar with the word "Molo". What does it mean?"

"It just means pier." Luigi replied. "It's a very old stone pier but it suits us for our business."

Fifteen minutes later, they reached the coast route and were presented with white sandy beaches and the blue water of the Adriatic.

"Wow," remarked Peg. "You are very lucky to live in such a beautiful part of the world. Do you come to the beach often?"

Luigi laughed. "No Magdalena, I don't. My security team would revolt if I made them stand in the hot sun while I was working on my tan. I prefer to do my laps in the pool at the villa where my guards can stand in the shade."

"Sounds reasonable," Peg responded. "But, please call me Maggi."

Forty-five minutes later, they arrived at Molo Audace and got out of the car. The pier was about 100 feet wide. There were small freighters tied up on each side. A crane was lifting pallets stacked with wooden crates from one ship to the other. Crews were working at either end loading and unloading the pallets.

"How long does it take to make the transfer?" Marc asked.

"About four hours." Luigi replied."

"Are you not concerned with customs inspectors catching you? It's broad daylight. I would think it safer to do the transfer at night." Peg interjected.

Luigi smiled. "We pay them to not be here when we're using the dock."

"This pier will not take a larger ship in case we decide to increase the size of the arms shipment. Do you have an alternate pier where a large ship can dock?" Marc asked.

"Yes," Luigi replied. "The next pier south will work but, there will be scheduling problems, as its more in use. There will also be higher fees which will cut into our profits."

"We believe, the increase in volume, say double, will more than offset any additional expenses." Marc said.

"That sounds good but, I need to look at the plan in greater detail before I can commit. And, of course, I need to present the plan to Don Giovanni for his approval. We'll discuss this more back at the Villa. Come, I want to introduce you to my lieutenant. He has been supervising the last shipment." Luigi called up to the men working on the deck of the ship that was being loaded. "Antonio, please come down. I want you to meet our American friends."

A swarthy man of about thirty broke from the group and deck and came down the gangway. He smiled as he approached — mostly at Peg. "Ciao Luigi." He said.

"Ciao Antonio," Luigi responded. "I present Magdalena Conti, or Maggi Conti and Pietro Romano. Our guests from the American Mafia."

Antonio took Peg's hand. "My pleasure, Signorina." He said, looking directly into her eyes.

"Pleased to meet you," Peg responded. She had to pull her hand to get him to release hers. Peg thought: *"what is it about Italian men that make me think, they are undressing me at the first meeting."*

Antonio tore his gaze from Peg and turned to Marc. "Ciao, Marc," he said as he shook Marc's hand.

"Ciao," Marc replied.

Luigi interjected: "Antonio, you will join us for dinner." An order, not a request."

"Certainly," he replied. "I will see you this evening." He turned and went back up the gangway.

"Antonio has been supervising all of our shipment this past year." Luigi explained. "His predecessor was killed in an ambush. We lost the whole shipment. Since then, we have put more men on the transfer in Syria. Under Antonio's supervision, we have not lost another load. There have been attacks but he is a strong leader and always wins through. Come, let's get back to the Villa for some lunch and quiet time this afternoon."

The return trip was spent detailing plans to double the volume of arms coming from the American Mafia. Marc and Peg agreed to procuring a larger vessel to hand the increase. Luigi would handle getting a large vessel on his end and setup moving to a larger pier. He would also need to increase the manpower to safeguard the convoys in Syria.

They had lunch on the patio again. It was light, minestrone and salad. After they finished their coffee, Luigi rose and asked to be excused. He turned to Marc. Will you join me?"

Marc replied: "Sure."

This suited Peg. She wanted to contact their Italian counter parts in the Italian Agency for External information (AISE) to give a status report. Believing that most rooms were bugged, she opted to go into the garden below the swimming pool. She dialed the cell number Alfredo Beloni had given them. He answered on the second ring. "Ciao, Peg or Marc?"

"Alfredo, it's Peg. "We have been taken in at face value. Everything is going to plan. Our next step is to accompany the next shipment to Syria. We'll look for weak spots where we can disrupt the arms flow. Their convoy has come under attack several times by rebel forces. These are random confrontations but, it makes me think that if we could organize a faction friendly to the US and, arm them, we have a good chance to consistently hijack the shipments and, we stand a chance they might give up the whole operation as a bad business deal."

"Sounds like a plan. Keep me informed. I will try to make a contact with other rebel groups for possibly carrying out your plan."

"Not sure we can accomplish that but, we'll keep our options open. The lieutenant supervising the shipments is very sharp, so we have to be careful."

"Okay, be safe. Ciao."

"Ciao," Peg replied.

Dinner was another feast. Starting with butternut squash bisque, a main course of lamb and a finish of creme brûle. Antonio, like Luigi, was fascinated with the States and New York. Conversation was a repeat of the previous evening. Luigi did not seem to mind. He smiled at Antonio's enthusiasm. Antonio was seated next to Peg. He was very animate as he spoke and touched her hand every-time he made a point. After dinner, they moved to the great room. Again, Luigi offered Armagnac and cigars. All took the

Armagnac—only Luigi chose the cigar. There were only three armchairs so, Peg took her place on a love seat. Antonio quickly moved to sit beside her.

"When is the next shipment going out?" Marc asked.

"In two days," Luigi replied. "We need to give Antonio a chance to rest and catch up with our plans. He's been managing back to back for a month now and he deserves a break."

"Will we be able to go on this next shipment?" Peg asked.

"Certainly," Luigi answered. "In fact, this is fortunate, one of our drivers is ill and we don't have a substitute. We weren't going to be able to shift his load to the other trucks. There's just not room. We would have to leave that truck at the port until the next shipment."

"We would be happy to help out," Marc said. "It would give us a better feel for the operation."

Luigi stood. "Marc. I would like to discuss some facets of our operation with you. Will you join me upstairs?"

"Sure," Marc smiled. He stood and followed Luigi out of the room.

"Ah, we're alone at last Antonio said.

"Yes, we are," Peg responded, in a neutral tone. "What would you like to talk about?"

"I wasn't thinking of talking," he replied leaning into her space.

"My, you Italian men sure like to make assumptions and move righ in." Peg said as she moved back.

"Mi scusi, but you are Italian too."

"Yes, I am. But I'm American Italian and we take things a bit more slowly in the States." She responded. "I think you are very nice and I am attracted to you but, I'd like to take this a little bit slower please. We've only just met today."

"It seems a life time to me but as you say; I will slow down."

Peg said: "Tell me about yourself. How did you come to be here with Luigi? You are pretty young to be second-in-command."

They talked until midnight. Antonio asked about her life in the States. She responded with a fabricated tail of growing up in the "Family" in New York and how she worked to a positio0n of responsibility not normally relegated to a woman.

When the clock struck 12, she rose. "Please excuse me. I'm still feeling jet lag so, I'll like to go to my room now."

Antonio stood up and took her hand—kissing the back. "I will see you to your room," he said.

At her door, he took her hand again and kissed it. "Buona notte. Good night. I'll see you at breakfast."

Peg locked her door and moved to the balcony using her satellite phone to give Langley and update on their plans. She knew Marc would stop by her room later so, she didn't undress but reclined on the bed with a book. Around 2 o'clock, there was a light knock on the door. She opened for Marc. "Hi, lover boy. Are you getting enough?"

"Whew", Marc answered. "That guy is a power house. I wish I could have met him under different circumstances. How are you doing with Antonio?"

"He's very aggressive," she responded. "I put him off for now. I'll gradually warm up to him. Or so he'll think. He is a talker and likes to brag. When we're on the ship, I should be able to learn more about their operation."

"Earlier, I contacted Langley and gave them a progress report. They say to get details about the Syria end of the operation. They think that if we can interrupt the flow there, the whole operation will die for lack of making a profit."

"Good morning," Luigi said as he entered the dining room.

Everyone responded in kind.

"What are your plans for today?" He continued.

Antonio spoke: "If you don't have something for me, I was going to take Maggi to Venezia. She wants to go shopping."

"No, these two days are for you to rest. If taking Maggi shopping is restful? By all means, do so." Luigi said.

Marc laughed. "Believe me, shopping with Maggi is anything but restful. So good luck on that."

Peg glared at Marc. She couldn't hold the stern face so she broke into laughter too.

"Marc, what would you like to do today?" Luigi asked.

"I would like to try my hand at falconry. I'd like you to show me around the area. Then I'd like to discuss the logistics of expanding your operation." Marc answered.

"Fine. We'll take a tour, have lunch and the we can discuss possible plans. I'm interested in how much your Family is willing to front and what percentage they are expecting."

"Antonio are you planning on lunch in the city?"

"Yes." Antonio responded. "We'll probably be back mid-after noon."

Luigi turned to Peg. "We will wait for you if you want to take part in our discussion."

"No that's not necessary. Marc and I have talked this over at length and we're of a similar mind. However, I would like to try the falconry too." She answered.

Antonio rose. "Maggi, if you are ready, I'll bring my car around and meet you at the front."

"Give me five minutes. I need to get my purse." She replied. Four minutes later, Peg opened the front door. She heard a roar and looked up see to a red Ferrari coming around the corner of the villa. *"Why does that not surprise me?" She though.*

On the drive to Venice, Antonio regaled Peg with all the wonders of the canaled city. Peg didn't mention that she had been there three times before. To bring that up, she knew he would press her to describe her visits. As the previous trips were CIA business, she would have to invent a series of lies. Better to remain silent.

Chapter 7

Venice, Italy

They stuck mostly to the shops near San Marcos Square. Peg bought a pair of heels and an evening gown she felt to be more appropriate for dinners at the villa.

As noon approached, Antonio said: "How about some lunch? I know a great restaurant off the square. It's hard to find but well worth the adventure."

"Sure," Peg replied. "I'm game."

"What is this word game? I don't think I've heard it before."

Peg laughed. "Game means, I'm willing to try something new."

"Bene," Antonio replied. "I can use that word on my friends." He took her arm and directed her down a small alley.

They walked for another hundred yards and crossed a narrow bridge spanning a small canal. Further on, two men stepped out of an alcove and blocked their path. They both held knives next to their legs.

Antonio quickly tore off his leather jacket and wrapped it around his left arm. Maggi get behind me!" He shouted.

"No," she replied. "Fan out. We'll each take one."

"you're crazy," Antonio said but he did as she requested.

What Antonio would soon learn was that Peg was proficient in martial art of Shaolin Chin Ma.

"Non vuoi farlo. "Sono tenete con la famiglia."   "You don't' want to do this. I'm a lieutenant in the Ndrangheta Family."

"Si, ma il morto capo ti vuole morto." "Yes, but our boss wants you dead."

Antonio broke into English. "They are serious, Maggi. Get behind me."

"No," she repeated. "I can handle this."

Both of the men rushed them with their knives extended.

Peg's opponent thrust toward her chest. She turned to the right and to the side allowing the blade to pass her. She grabbed the wrist behind the knife, with her right hand and the elbow on that arm with her left hand. Applying upward pressure to the elbow, she twisted the knife hand down and turned the knife into her adversary's body. He screamed and dropped the knife. She lifted his elbow higher and shoved his hand behind his back forcing him to kneel. She rapped the knuckles of her left hand hard against his temple. He dropped like a stone — a dead stone.

Antonio was sparring with his opponent by deflecting the knife thrusts with his jacket. Neither of them could get the upper hand. When his adversary heard his partner scream, he glanced over to see him drop.

Peg moved to assist Antonio and the other assailant broke off and ran. He disappeared down an alley and was soon out of sight.

"Fantastico!" Antonio exclaimed. "Where did you learn that?"

"In our Family, all women know how to take care of themselves."

"Let's wake up your guy and find out what's going on. According to the tattoo on his arm, they are from the Gambini Family. They are our competition in the drug business."

"He's not going to be able to talk," she said. "He's dead."

"Then, we need to get out of here. Are you still up for lunch?"

"Sure," she replied. "I worked up and appetite." She slipped her arm around his as they walked away.

"Shit." Antonio remarked. "This was my favorite jacket," he said as he dropped the shredded garment into a trash barrel.

"Well, we are here to shop and as you are going into women's shops, I guess I can go with you to a men's shop."

"First we have lunch." Antonio said.

They found an open-air restaurant on the Grand Canal. They both opted for seafood paired with a crisp bottle of Pinot Grigio.

True to Peg's word, it was shops in the plural. She was able to find several light weight dresses suitable for the climate here and some rougher clothes for the truck ride coming up in Syria. At an exclusive men's shop, they found a suitable replacement for Antonio's jacket.

Several hours later they took a water taxi to the parking garage outside the city. The drive back was pleasant, and Antonio pressed Peg for more stories of America — mostly New York city.

Chapter 8

VILLA del FALCO

Friuli-Venezia Giulia, Italy

Marc and Luigi finished their morning coffee. When Carlo came to clear the service, Luigi asked him to send four men to the aviary to act as beaters for their hunt.

"Marc," Luigi said. "I'm sure you don't have proper clothes for this sport. We are of a size so I think some of my clothes will fit you."

Marc followed Luigi to his bedroom where he selected some sturdy pants, some well-worn boots and a hunting jacket. Handing the clothes to Marc, he said" "Meet me at the front entrance is fifteen minutes."

"Thanks. I'll be there." Marc replied.

As they walked down the front stairs, Luigi spoke. "I want to show you my horses. I usually do my falconry from horse back so I can cover more ground but today, we'll be walking if that's okay with you."

Marc replied: "Sure. I'd like to walk."

Reaching the stables, Luigi pulled open the stable door and with a wave of his hand, ushered Marc into the dim interior. There were rows of six stalls on each side but only four of the stalls was occupied. All were dark horses. Luigi stopped at each horse to rub their muzzle and offer a sugar cube. Marc noticed that he was emotionally attached to his mounts. He thought: *"This guy is a big softy."*

"I enjoy riding. If you are interested, we can pack a picnic lunch and I'll take you on a tour of the villa's grounds."

"That would be great," Marc replied.

"Good," Luigi said. "On to the mews then."

They walked for hundred yards more before they came to a small building with several walk-in sized cages attached. "I like to keep the birds away from the car and truck noises, so we've built the mews out here. They don't respond to loud noises, Particularly Antonio's Ferrari."

There were four men standing near the entrance to the mews. They were dressed in rugged clothing and each carried a six-foot pole.

"Why the poles," Marc asked.

"These men will beat the brush to stir up the game." Luigi explained.

Marc followed Luigi into the interior of the mews. Each of the cages had a separate indoor roosting and feeding area. Two of the cages were occupied outside the building.

With surprise in his voice, Marc exclaimed: "Wow, they are huge. What kind of birds are these?"

"They are golden eagles," Luigi responded. "They are able to bring down rabbits of course and even small deer or cinghiale — how you say in English?"

"Boar," Marc injected.

"Yes. If we're lucky, we may capture a boar today, but count on rabbit as dinner. That's our best bet."

They entered the building from bright sunlight to a dim interior. The walls were lined with falconry equipment including several large gloves that would extend from hand to elbow. Luigi gave a sharp whistle and both birds flew in and settled on the interior roosts. He slowly approached each bird and fitted a falcon hood on the falcons. Luigi select two gloves handing one to Marc. "This should fit you fine."

Marc slid the glove over his arm mimicking Luigi.

"Now do as I do." Luigi said. He positioned his arm at one of the bird's legs and the falcon stepped onto his wrist Marc copied his actions.

"Wow!" Marc exclaimed. "He's much lighter than he looks."

"Yes," Luigi replied. "Their bones are hollow which allows them to fly. If they had bones like a mammal, they'd never get off the ground."

"Shall we hunt?" Luigi opened the door and ushered Marc through.

They walked for several hundred feet and stopped near a large stand of trees and brush. There was an open field on the far side. "Remove the hood then raise your arm sharply like this." Luigi demonstrated. Marc followed his lead and both eagles flew to the top of the trees.

"Andiamo!" Luigi shouted at the beaters. The men, staying about fifteen feet apart, moved through the brush swinging their poles. Shortly, they could hear something moving away from them toward the open field. Vison was obscured by the bushes so they couldn't tell what they had spooked, but both eagles swooped down and grabbed their prey. Two of the men dropped their poles and rushed to where the birds had their catch pinned. Drawing knives, they quickly slashed open the game allowing the eagles to feed on the entrails.

Luigi and Marc broke free of the bushes. "Una sorpresa!" "A surprise!" Luigi exclaimed. He continued in English: "Both a young boar and a small roe deer. This is magnificent hunting for your first time. You bring me luck!"

Marc was smiling broadly as Luigi wrapped an arm around his shoulder and pulled him close. Marc looked up to stare directly into Luigi's eyes. "I learn from the master."

"Come," Luigi said. "We need to collect the birds." He moved to one of the eagles and lowered his arm to let the bird settle on his wrist Marc copied his moves Luigi covered his eagle with its hood and Marc followed suit.

Using their poles, the men fashioned carriers for the game and followed Marc and Luigi back to the falcon shed. Once the eagles were secured and fed more of the entails, they walked back to the villa.

"We will have the venison tonight. The boar takes longer to cook properly so we'll have that tomorrow night." Luigi remarked.

Guiding Marc to the bottom of the stairs, Luigi took his arm and pressed lightly. "Now is quiet time. Rest and refresh yourself and we meet for cocktails at seven". He turned and went into his study.

Marc was resting in his room and trying to put together a plan of disrupting the next deliver to ISIS. Nothing was coming together–not with only two days for the next trip to Syria. He had a few ides, but nothing that could be setup in this time frame. The best He could do was just go on this trip and look for weak spots. *"Maybe"*, he thought, *"Peg could see something he'd missed."*

The roar of Antonio's Ferrari announced their return from shopping. Marc waited until he heard Peg's door open and close. Moving quietly across the hall, he rapped softly on her door.

Peg opened the door and motioned him without speaking. She waved to the balcony. Speaking softly, she gave a recap of time in Venice and the attack by the Gambini Family.

Marc said: "I haven't been able to come up with a plan to disrupt the flow of the arms. This could give us another option. If the Gambini Family is strong enough, we might interest them in hijacking the shipment before or after it leaves Italy. We should contract our Italian friends, Beloni or Cervelli, to see if they have any leverage with that Family. The only thing I've come up with so far is to go on this next trip and look for weak spots somewhere in their operation. Maybe we can come at this from another angle. On the possibility of an air strike, it's too high a risk. Even knowing when and where the strike would be, may not give us enough time to get away from the caravan."

"Let me get the secure phone our Italian friends gave us and take a walk in the garden," Peg said.

A Few minute later Peg keyed in the number they were given. On the second ring; "Ciao, this is Beloni, who am I speaking with?"

"It's Peg O'Ryan Alfredo, nice talking to you. We need some intel on the Gambini Family here in the Venice area. We are looking at a scenario of disrupting the arms flow by having the shipment hijacked either on land or at sea after their ship leaves port."

"I know of the Gambini Family. They have an ongoing feud with the Nuova Mala Del Brenta. It's a possibility, but the only incentive for them would be keeping the arms. I don't think my government would go along with giving the Gambini Family that much fire power."

"Didn't see that one coming," Peg responded.

"Let's not let go of your idea just yet." Beloni said. "Perhaps if your government would be willing to buy the arms, we could make it work.

"Good thought. I'll pass the idea by Peter and see what he thinks." Peg answered.

"When does the next shipment leave Italy?" Beloni asked.

"Two days." Peg responded.

"Don't think we can work in that time frame." Beloni said.

"Okay," Peg said. "we are going along on this next shipment to Syria to look for weak spots in their operation. This gives us a two-prong attack. Let's take two days to work this plan and talk again."

"That works for me. Ciao Peg." Beloni disconnected.

"It's late night at Langley," Marc said. "I'll call Peter tomorrow." Cocktails are at seven so let's get some rest." Marc went to the doorway, opening it, he looked up and down the and crossed silently to his room.

At 6:45 that the evening. Marc knocked on Peg's door. Peg answered the door wearing one of her new outfits.

"Wow," Marc exclaimed. "Who are you trying to impress?"

Peg did a 360-degree twirl. "I was thinking of getting a little closer to Antonio, but that's already a done deal the way he was crowding me while we were shopping. So now it just to look my best at dinner. You are looking pretty sharp yourself."

Marc was wearing tan slacks, a burgundy shirt and a linen jacket. The shirt was open three buttons. Marc cocked his arm to Peg. "Shall we?"

Looping her arm through Marc's, Peg replied: "We shall."

As they approached the great room, they could hear Antonio's loud description of the conflict with two of the Gambini men. He stopped talking when they entered the room.

"Good evening," Luigi said. "Antonio has been known to embellish some of his tales, but this time, I'm inclined to believe him."

"I thought we had told you we are students of Shaolin Chin Na. If not, I apologize. All the soldiers in our Family are trained in this martial art style. We believe it's better to take out an opponent quietly rather than resorting to a loud gun." Peg said.

"My men and I would like a demonstration if you please," Luigi asked.

Peg and Marc exchanged looks.   "Sure, we could do that," Peg responded.

"Great, Luigi replied. "How about 10 tomorrow morning?"

"Sounds good," Peg answered.

"Now, your drinks. It was gin and tonic for Magdalena and scotch neat for Pietro, right?" Peg and Marc nodded.

"Enough of that. Did Pietro tell you about our good fortune with the eagles?"

Peg shook her head. Marc said: "Haven't had time."

"Bene." Luigi said and preceded to regale Peg with their morning's luck. "So, we are having venison tonight and boar tomorrow."

Chapter 9

Villa del Falco

Friuli-Venezia Giulia, Italy

Next Morning

Next morning after breakfast, Peg and Marc were in the   garden. Peg was talking to Peter on her secure phone. "What's the answer on using the Gambini Family to disrupt the flow of arms?"

"Both of our governments will not go along with just another mafia Family taking over the arms shipping." Peter said. "We need to proceed with the original plan. We need to interrupt the arms exchange to a point that the operation is no longer profitable for the Nuova Mala Del Brenta Family."

"Okay Peter," Peg responded. "We should be on the road, somewhere in Syria, with this next shipment in a few days. We'll call again with an update."

Peg turned to Marc. "That went as I expected but you never know we've seen weirder things pass as okay. Now we can concentrate on the original plan."

"Fine with me," Marc replied. "Look who's coming."

Peg looked up to see Luigi and Antonio striding toward

them.

Luigi had a stern look and asked: "Who were you talking to?"

"I was talking to our Don giving him and up to date on what has transpired and what is planned for this next shipment. And I told him about the Gambini Family's attack on Antonio and I," Peg answered. He is happy with our plans and interested but not concerned with the attack in Venice. Did you want to talk to us?" Peg asked.

Luigi seemed to be mollified. "Antonio wanted to show the gymnasium and ask about any things you might want for the demonstration."

They walked around the villa to another building near the pool. What looked like a pool house turn out to be that and a fairly large gymnasium.

"Pool house is for summer and gymnasium is for winter. Will this be okay and do you need anything special?" Luigi said.

"We could use some loose-fitting cloths." Marc replied.

Antonio walked them over to a cabinet and opened the doors. Marc saw various sizes of gym cloths and martial arts sparing outfits. He turned to Luigi. "I'm impressed. Who is into martial arts?"

"That would be primarily Antonio and me." Luigi replied. "Lately it's been just me. With Antonio guarding the shipments I don't have anyone to spar with. I've tried to get some of the men interested but I believe they think that if they hurt me, they might disappear. Perhaps you will indulge me?"

Marc smiled. "I think I smell a trap. You are going to size me up at our demonstration–learn my moves and then waste me if I spar with you."

Luigi laughed. "Now, why would I do that?" Luigi looked at his watch. "Antonio, it's near ten. Roundup some of the men are that not on duty, and have them come to the gymnasium."

Turning to the duo he said: "Pick out your sparing outfits and you can change in the pool house."

Peg and Marc came into the gymnasium, from the locker room, to find Luigi reclining on the bleachers.

"We will start as soon as my men get here." Luigi said.

"Okay," Marc replied. He and Peg moved onto the mat and ran through a series of stretching exercises. About fifteen minutes later, twenty men filed in and took seats in the bleachers.

"You can start anytime," Luigi said.

"Okay," Marc replied. "If you are not familiar with Chin Na, let me just say as an introduction what we are going to do. Although Chin Na is based in Kung Fu, the focus is on body areas and extremities. We will be pulling our strikes as following through could result in injuries."

Peg and Marc moved onto the center of the mat. They bowed to each other and quickly moved into attack/defense positions. They both moved into each other and began trading blows aimed at chest or head targets. Neither were able to land a hit. Marc stepped back and putting weigh on his left foot, dipped and spun to deliver a blow to Peg's head. Instead of moving out of the strike area, Peg moved in capturing Marc's right ankle with her left hand. Pulling his body in, she delivered a flat handed strike to Marc's chest. She released his leg and Marc slammed into the mat on his back. Peg rushed forward to deliver a kick to his head. Marc rolled and captured her back leg. Twisting his legs, he threw Peg to the mat. Both moved back into the attack/defense positions.

They sparred for another half hour, neither getting an upper hand. Because Marc had a longer reach, he thrust his flat right-handed move to Peg's throat. Peg did not try to block the move. She let his arm slide past. Grasping his wrist with her right hand and his elbow with her left, she pushed his arm down with her right hand and shove his elbow up Marc's fingers slammed into his own ribs. Peg release his arm and Marc stepped back crossed his wrists, signifying the match was over. Marc added: "That last move is used if the opponent is thrusting with a knife. From what Peg tells me, that's the defense move she used on the Gambini soldier. What did you think of it Antonio?"

"To tell the truth, it happened so fast, I didn't see what Maggi did, and I was busy with my guy." Antonio responded.

Luigi started clapping and shortly his men followed suit. "Bene, bene. I am impressed. Cool down and take a shower. Come to the patio. Lunch should be ready."

Chapter 10

Villa del Falco

Friuli-Venezia Giulia, Italy

Afternoon

Lunch was barbequed chicken and asparagus, paired with a Pinot Grigio.

As par, the conversation was light – mostly Peg and Marc answering questions about New York. This time, Antonio seemed to be interest in Chicago.

"America is such a large country how many Families are there?"

"About sixty-three," Marc answered. "That number fluctuates as some Families are absorbed by stronger Families and/or a Family takes over another city where there are several gangs with no central command. There is a council made up of a Family member. Usually the Dons, but sometimes the second-in-command. Much like Luigi. They loosely agree to respect boundaries, an act as committee to arbitrate disputes."

"Let's move to my office. I'll have Antonio describe what our procedures are and what you can expect on the caravan ride. Antonio?"

"Well first, we've had a delay. Something has gone wrong with the ship's engine. An oil leak, the chief mechanic says it will take two days to repair. We've sent a message to the people in charge of the trucks to hold at the port. It takes most of two days to offload the arms and load them on the trucks. There will be five trucks. Each truck has a driver and a man riding along with an automatic rifle. There is also a rifle for the driver. We've not had a lot of trouble but sometimes splinter gangs try to capture one or more trucks. If we present a strong response, they usually back off."

Marc asked: "Does the caravan move in day light or at night?"

"Both," Antonio replied. "Depending on logistics, once the trucks are loaded, we do not stop until we reach Homs."

"How long is the trip?" Peg asked.

"It's 150 kilometers so about four hours. The driver and the guard will trade off driving."

Carlo came into the room and whispered in Luigi's ear. Luigi nodded and dismissed his man-servant.

"The chief mechanic called. When he got deeper into the repair, he believes the break down was sabotage. I can't discern what the point would be in causing us a two-day delay." Luigi said. "I'll have to think on this for a while."

"Anyway, Magdalena did you want to see the eagles?"

"Please. I'd like that very much.' Peg responded.

The foursome walked down to the falconry. The pair were in the outside cage.

"They are so large." Peg said in a voice of awe. "I'm not sure I'm strong enough to let one settle on my arm."

Luigi laughed. "Come inside the falconry. I think you will be surprised." He opened the door and ushered Peg in.

Luigi whistled and both birds flew to their interior roosts. "Here, Magdalena, put this glove on." He showed her how to bring the glove next to the eagle's legs. The eagle hopped into the glove. Peg was startled but held her arm firm.

"Wow," she exclaimed. "They really are light."

The three men chuckled.

"Move your arm near the roost and give a little lift." The eagle resumed its position on the bar. "Now we must reward her because we didn't take her on a flight." Luigi opened a stainless bucket and gave each of the birds a piece of chicken.

"How do you know it's a she." Peg asked.

"Females are slightly smaller than males." Luigi replied.

Luigi directed them out of the falconry. "Let's go back to the main house for some rest time and we'll meet for cocktails at seven."

Chapter 11

Villa del Falco

Friuli-Venezia Giulia, Italy

That Evening

Over cocktails, the conversation again revolved around the states. "Tell us about San Francisco and Los Angeles." Antonio asked.

Marc replied. "For some reason they are called sister cities, but they couldn't be more different. San Francisco is all hills surrounded by water and very compact. Los Angeles is sprawled out and runs from the ocean to mountains. Because the original founders of San Francisco were Italian, the Families are very strong there. In Los Angeles, the one Family takes back seat to the black and Latino gangs."

"But the weather is much nicer there. Right?" Antonio asked.

"For sure." Peg chimed in. "The most noticeable difference is the humidity. Where the eastern seaboard and middle America have high humidity, the western coast has very low humidity. Snow is far to the east for both cities."

Carlo appeared at the doorway and announced dinner was ready.

As promised, dinner was cinghiale over papradelle with side of sautéed spinach and finger potatoes. The meal was paired with a robust chianti.

"I've never has boar. This is wonderful," Peg exclaimed. "This is wonderful."

"Pleased you like it," Luigi replied. "It's a common dish in Italy. I'm happy to have introduced it to you. Let's go to the great room for some after dinner drinks."

Once seated, Luigi said: "you must try this other Armagnac. It's very old and very smooth." Both Peg and Marc nodded. Antonio smiled as if he was being treated special.

The duo each sipped the liquor. Both smiled.

"Glad you like it. This Armagnac is my personal favorite. I …." Luigi paused Carlo as rushed into the room.

"Signore Luigi! Signore Luigi! There is trouble at the dock. They have been attacked. Two of our men are dead and some of the cargo has been taken."

"Merda!" Luigi exclaimed. "Carlo, have the limousine brought to the front. Pietro, Magdalena arm yourselves. Antonio, bring two automatic rifles. You will drive. We meet at the front door in five minutes."

Chapter 12

Molo Audace

Friuli-Venezia Giulia, Italy

Antonio, a skilled driver, chose a more direct route and they made it to the pier in half the time as when they went along the coast. He drove down the pier and stopped at the gangplank. The four quickly exited the limo.

A man was standing at the ship's railing. He quickly came down the gangplank. He was sweating and wringing his hands. "Padrone there was nothing I could do. When I heard the shoots, I hid in the engine room. I did not have a gun."

"That's okay Nico. You did the correct thing. I would not like losing another man. Were you able to see them?"

"No Padrone. They were all dressed in black and they had black hoods."

"How much of the arms did they take?" Luigi asked.

"I'm not sure Padrone. They only had one truck that I could see."

"Antonio go have a look and see how much we have lost." Luigi directed.

Luigi then walked over to each of the guards and checked their necks for a pulse.

Peg and Marc stood back. "What do you want us to do?" Marc asked.

"Nothing for now." Luigi responded. "Before we left the villa, I directed one of my men to get three others and bring a van. They should be here soon."

Peg asked: "Do you have any idea who did this?"

"Yes. I'm pretty sure it was the Gambini Family. They have been pressuring me to allow them to join us on this venture. We don't need them and it would mean lower profits for us, and I've told them no several times. I can't let this go. If I did, we would appear weak. What I will do is try to recover the arms and take out three of their men. I don't want to start a full-scale war, but three for two is more of a reprimand."

The van arrived and pulled up behind the limousine. Antonio directed them to take the bodies and hose down the blood spillage.

"Why haven't the police arrived?" Marc asked.

"No one in this area will call the police. They don't want to get involved and I pay the police to stay away." Luigi replied.

Antonio came down the gangplank. "They didn't take too much; about half a van's worth. They must have been on a time schedule thinking the police would arrive sooner rather than later."

"There's not much we can do here tonight. Let's head back to the Villa. I'll address this tomorrow." Luigi said.

The ride back was at a slower pace and mostly in silence. Each seemed to be going over in their minds what had transpired and what the next step would be.

Chapter 13

Villa del Falco

Friuli-Venezia Giulia, Italy

Next Morning

There was a somber atmosphere hovering over coffee and breakfast the next morning. Breaking his rule of no business over meals, Luigi and Antonio were going through different scenarios to address dealing with the Gambini Family. Antonio was quite vocal over the form of retaliation they should take. He wanted an attack on their Gambini compound. Luigi was in favor of a limited strike.

"If we escalate this matter, beyond an appropriate level, we risk going into a full-blown war and our business will suffer." Luigi said. "A direct attack will result in more losses. Need I remind you we might not be able to guard the villa and sent enough men to keep the arms caravan safe."

Antonio frowned. "I understand. But we must do something."

Carlo came into the room and stood quietly with his hand clasped in front.

Luigi motioned for him to speak. "Signore, c'è un uomo qui per vedere voi. Dice di essere stato mandato da don Gambini." "Signore, there is a man to see you. He says he was sent by Don Gambini."

Everyone at the table exchanged glances of surprise.

"Okay let's go to the great room. Carlo, fa 'entrare l'uomo." "Carlo show the man in." Luigi said.

The four quickly moved to the room across the hall and took seats.

Carlo entered the room followed by a large man dressed in a very expensive suit. He carried a briefcase. "Signore this is the man that wanted to see you." He stepped away and the man moved forward.

"Don Visconti sono Mario Campo. Lieutenant a Don Gambini." "Don Visconti I am Mario Campo. Lieutenant to Don Gambini."

"Please speak English. Our guests are American." Luigi said. "And I'm not the Don; just first lieutenant."

"Si Signore. Don Gambini wants to express his deepest regrets for what happened last night. He says to tell you he did not authorize the raid. It was a rogue

Lieutenant who has been trying to take over the Family. He felt that this raid would show him to be a stronger leader." He presented the briefcase and opened it to show a large amount of money. "He wants the Families of the two we killed to have this. He told me to say, he does not believe that two-hundred-thousand Euros can replace the lives of the two men, but he hopes it will help. He also told me to say that the men responsible have been remove permanently." The man fell silent.

Luigi stayed quiet for which seemed several minutes. He did not show his anger. "Tell Don Gambini his apology is accepted."

"Grazie Signore. The arms are in a truck outside." The man turned and left the room.

"Antonio have one of the men take the arms back to the ship. Have everything ready to sail tomorrow morning."

"Magdalena, Pietro does that work for you?"

Peg and Marc exchange glances and each nodded to Luigi.

"Good. Breakfast will only be coffee. There will be plenty of food on the ship. The ship sails at 6 AM. We should all get some rest. It's late and morning will come soon enough."

Antonio turned to Peg. "Magdalena will you sit with me for a while?"

"Yes, but not for long. I want to be at my best tomorrow if we run into any more problems." Peg had a good idea what Antonio wanted to talk about. She was not disappointed.

"Shall we sit over here?" Antonio pointed to the love seat.

They both sat down and Antonio took Peg's hand. "I find you very attractive," Antonio spoke softly. You don't seem to like me much."

"Not so," Peg said. "It's been my experience that Italian men move too fast. Maybe it's because I'm American Italian, that I prefer some courting before I get involved. I'm not into one-night stands. We will have plenty of time to learn about each other on the ship." Peg rose and Antonio followed. He took her hand and kissed the back side.

"I will wait until we know each other. But I hope I don't have to wait too long."

Peg smiled at him tugging bit to draw her hand back. I'm going to bed now."

Antonio returned the smile. "Buona notte Magdalena."   "Good night."

Chapter 14

Villa del Falco

Friuli-Venezia Giulia, Italy

Next morning

Peg and Marc walked into the dining room at 5:20. Luigi and Antonio were seated and drinking coffee.

"Good morning Magdalena, Pietro." Luigi greeted the duo. "I hope you slept well. The ship is loaded and only awaits you three. Have some coffee and we will head to the pier. Carlo." He called out.

Carlo stepped into the room.

Fai portare la limousine al fronte. Per favore. ""Have the limousine brought around to the front. PLease."

"Si Signore," Carlo responded.

"I'll be coming to the pier see you off." Luigi said. Fifteen minutes later, they were headed down the coast.

Soon they pulled onto the pier. Exiting the limousine, Luigi shook Peg and Antonio hands. Marc, he pulled into an embrace. Be careful."

They pulled their luggage out of the trunk and the three climbed the gangplank. The crew pulled in the gangplank and the ship moved away. Luigi watched the ship until it was far out to sea. He gave a sigh and climbed back into the car.

Chapter 15

At Sea

The duo had not been on the ship before, so they were surprised to see a large lounge with comfortable seating, a dining table and chairs.

"Very nice," Peg remarked. "This can't be standard for a freight ship."

"No, it's not." Antonio replied. I spend so much time on board, Luigi decided that I needed a perk. There is only so much eating, sleeping and watching the waves, so this is to keep me sane."

Both Peg and Marc laughed.

"How long to the Syrian coast?" Marc asked.

"Four days, assuming good weather," Antonio responded. "Now, I have someone to play cards with. That and reading." He pointed to book case that held forty to fifty books. Fortunately, we have an excellent cook on board so we won't be eating gruel. Which reminds me, we will be having breakfast soon. Bring your bags and I'll show you to your cabins."

The duo picked up their bags and followed Antonio down a flight of stairs.

"Where are your bags," Peg asked.

"Everything I need is here." Antonio answered. "There is a steward who cleans the cabins daily and takes care of laundry."

Antonio stopped in the hallway and opened two doors opposite. "The cabins are identical, so take your pick, and refresh yourselves. Meet me back in the lounge. Breakfast will be in fifteen minutes."

Peg and Marc went to their cabins and unpacked. They met in the hallway. "We need to give Peter an update, but we're ten hours ahead, so it'll have to wait. I don't think our phones will work in the cabin so we'll have to chance making the call up on the deck." Peg said. "Let's head to the lounge."

Breakfast wasn't as elaborate as at the villa, but it was satisfying.

"Can you give us a rundown of what will happen after we dock at Latakia," Marc asked"

"Sure," Antonio replied. "What I'm going to lay out for you is what has been planned, not what might happen. Remember this Syria. The port is not that busy, but it's a small pier and sometimes we have to wait for space. Keeping that in mind, we can only accommodate two trucks on the pier at the same time. As the pier is narrow, we need to back the trucks down the pier to the ship. We figure if there is a problem, we'd prefer the trucks be empty. There would be a delay for another truck. Better losing a truck rather than losing a truck and the arms."

"Homs is not that far, only one-hundred and fifty kilometers but the roads are not in very good condition, so we won't be able to drive any faster than thirty-five mile per hour. There are no check points. Again, this is Syria so if the road is blocked, we have a problem. I will be carrying ten-thousand Euros for bribery. That's if the ones doing the road block are small-time bandits, they would rather have money than arms. And, they know taking the arms would be an affront to ISIS. Something that ISIS would not let slide. If it's another group in direct competition with ISIS, we have a different problem. They will want the arms. Decision point. We can try to fight our way through or let them have the arms. We've never lost a shipment. When they see how heavily we're armed, they usually back off."

The trio settled into a pattern of breakfast, lunch and dinner interspersed with reading and cards.

The second night, Peg kept Antonio busy while Marc went out on the deck to phone Peter. He filled him in on the time schedule for reaching Homs. He admitted to not having a plan. He told Peter that they'd play it by ear but doubted they have a chance to disrupt this particular shipment.

Chapter 16

Latakia, Syria

The trio were on the bridge as they approached the harbor in Latakia. Antonio had a pair of binoculars and was scanning the pier.

"Looks like we won't have a wait to unload our cargo. There doesn't seem to be any unusual activity."

It took them another half hour before the ship was secured at the dock. There were two trucks already on the pier.

"I'll need you two to stand guard on the upper deck of the ship. You will be able to spot any potential trouble. There are automatic weapons in a cabinet in the lounge. Keep them with you as we might need them on the journey to Homs. I usually don't do this but I should be able to speed up the loading of trucks."

It went pretty much as Antonio had described. The pier was narrow and the backing of the trucks on the pier went slowly. It took close to six hours before the arms were transferred to the trucks. As each truck was being loaded, the ship steward put a container of food and water in each cab. All the other drivers were Italian and none seemed to speak English. Antonio was giving the men last minute instructions. Peg and Marc were able to understand mostly but could not catch every word.

Antonio motioned Peg and Marc down to the pier as the last truck was being loaded. When they met up with Antonio, he had just finished talking to the drivers and guards. Turning to the duo, he beckoned them to come nearer. "I will be in the lead truck and I'd like you two to take the third one. Barring any surprises, we should be Ohms in three to four hours. ISIS will provide the manpower to unload the truck. They insist on this so they can inspect each crate.   That's okay with me as we'll be inspecting each container of opium. Call it mutual distrust, but it's necessary."

"What happens next?" Peg asked.

"We turn right around and head back to the ship. Homs is under siege on the east side of the city.

There's no telling when it might spread to the west side. The reason for the food and water in each truck is so we can get out of Homs as fast as we can. Our cargo will fit in one truck which will be mine. It has a value, not as much as the weapons, but the risk of a hijacking is greater. The other drivers and guards have a compound in Latakia where they and the trucks will wait for our next shipment. We'll move out of Latakia as soon as possible."

The steward will have dinner waiting for us."

The guards and driver were standing in a group waiting on instructions for Antonio. He turned to them. "Tutti ai loro camion. Ci stiamo trasferendo ora." "Everyone to their trucks. We are moving out now. Even though Peg and Marc could not totally understand what Antonio was saying, they followed the lead of the men as they headed to the trucks and followed suit.

Chapter 17

On the M1 road to Homs, Syria

The road was paved to the outskirts of Latakia and then turned to dirt. The caravan slowed down as the best way to deal with rocks and potholes. Marc was driving. Peg sat next to him with the automatic weapon across her lap.

"Christ!" Marc exclaimed. "This is not a road it's a goat path. Be sure the safety is on that weapon and please aim it away from me." Marc's weapon was standing up right between the seats. "And make sure my gun's safety is on too. It would be embarrassing to shoot the top out of the tuck."

Peg chuckled. "Yeah. It would shoot our tough Mafia image down real fast."

The road seemed to be following and old river bed with near vertical cliffs on both sides. Peg was scanning to each side and trying to look ahead but couldn't see much due to the dust kicked up by the trucks in front.

"I hope it's not like this all the way to Homs. This terrain is perfect for an ambush."

The road emerged from the river bed to rolling sand hills. A brisk wind was blowing from the right side so they were soon able to see further head. Not far though as the road curve between the hills.

The road was barely wide enough for one truck. There were pull over spaces for navigating past other vehicles.

Each side of the road was dry vegetation. Every so often there were breaks in the bushes. From the hoof prints, they appeared to be goat paths.

There was no air conditioning so it was stifling in the cab of the truck. They had been traveling for hour. Peg opened the box of food and water and pulled out a flask. She took a drink and passed it to Marc. "Gag." Marc said. "That tastes like piss."

"Now how would you know that unless you're a gold shower queen?" Peg responded.

"Very funny." Marc replied. "And what does it taste like to you?"

Peg laughed. "we will now change the subject."

Marc chuckled. "Okay, truce."

They were rounding a curve when the lead trucks came to an abrupt stop. The road was blocked by a large truck and a jeep across the road. There were half dozen men behind the vehicles. They had weapons resting on the hoods of the vehicles. Ahead, they could see Antonio and the driver exiting his truck. He had a satchel under his left arm, his right hand rested on the pistol at his right side.

Marc said. "Bring your weapon, with the safety off, and let's see what's going on. Walk slowly and keep your gun pointed down."

"Right," Peg answered.

They came up behind Antonio. Without turning his head, he spoke. "Move to either side of us. Hold your weapons across your chests. These men are just bandits. My driver speaks

Arabic. They will probably understand him."

"Chiedi loro quello che vogliono." "Ask them what they want."

"Madha turid?" "What do you want?" The driver shouted.

The men behind the truck and jeep seemed to be discussing what to do next. Finally, one responded to the driver.

"yjb 'an tadfae liaistikhdam tariqina. "You must pay to use our road."

He translated for Antonio. "Dicono chiedi loro quello che vogliono." "They say, there is a fee to use their road."

Antonio translated for Peg and Marc. "They want money to use their road. To his driver he directed. "Quanto?" "How much?"

The driver spoke to the men. Again, they seemed to discuss the amount. Their leader replied.

The driver said to Antonio, "Duecento euros." "Two-hundred Euros."

Antonio did not translate for the duo. He said to the driver, "Cento euro. Questo è tutto ciò che ho." "One hundred. That's all I have."

The driver relayed the amount to the men. They responded with their agreement. Antonio opened the satchel and handed the driver the cash and motioned him to take it to the bandits. He hesitated. Antonio spoke sharply to him and he reluctantly walked over to them, stopping short of the jeep. A man came around the jeep and grabbed the money and shouted to his team. They mounted the vehicles and drove away.

"Why didn't you give the full two-hundred euros?" Peg asked. "It's a small amount to avoid a confrontation."

"These people don't need guns, they need food." Antonio replies. "If I gave into their demands, it would make us look weak and they'd be waiting for us on the next trip. They could see that we have weapons and they're not sure who would win a fight. Okay everyone, Andiamo!" "Let's go!"

They front trucks were moving by the time the duo got back to their truck. "I can see why Luigi relies on Antonio so much, he's pretty sharp." Peg said.

"Yeah," Marc responded. "He most likely knows about the whole operation. See what you can learn."

"Will do," Peg replied. "He likes to brag, so I'll just need to stroke his ego and we should get some good intel. Problem is, to get him to stop talking."

Marc laughed.

Chapter 18

Homs, Syria

There were no more causes for delay and they rolled into the outskirts of Homs. The caravan came to a halt at a barricade. Antonio and his driver exited their truck and approached the line of vehicles. Peg and Marc had climbed down from their truck to see what was going on. They could see Antonio talking; his driver translating. They returned to their truck as the barricade opened. Peg and Marc fallowed suit. Fifteen minutes later they entered an industrial compound. A man was standing at the entrance to a warehouse and directed them to pull inside. The building was large and the caravan halted in line.

A swarm of men approached the trucks and started to unload them. Within half Hour, the trucks were empty and the crates were being opened. Antonio and his drivers stood off to the side until the last of the weapons and ammunition were spread out on the floor. One man had a manifest and was ticking off items. This took another half hour.

He stopped and came over to Antonio. He spoke in English. "Everything is in order. Please inspect our product."

Peg and Marc had come up to Antonio to observe the interchange. They followed Antonio and the Syrian over to a row of open crates. Each crate was filled to the brim with plastic bags holding what appeared to be white powder.

Antonio motioned Peg and Marc over to the crates. "If you help me with this it will go a lot faster. Take your knives and make small punctures in bags at random and not just the bags on top. Taste the heroin for purity. You've done this before?"

Both Peg and Marc nodded. The duo had tasted heroin before, but on a very limited basis. They were not experts, so they were going to have to wing it hoping Antonio didn't start questioning them too closely.

This took about an hour. Both were starting to feel the effects; Antonio didn't seem to be affected. He was watching Peg and Marc and decide to call a halt to the sampling. "You're not use to this, are you?"

Peg answered. "Not this much at one time."

"Don't worry about it. This more for show. They need arms and ammunition more than we need their cocaine. At least that's what we've led them to believe. They think if we caught them trying to screw us that would the end of the shipments to them.

We've let them know that there are other buyers and the only reason we stick with them is the quality of their product."

Marc laughed. "You could have said something earlier. I do not like getting high."

Peg echoed his sentiments.

Antonio chuckled. "Sorry. I was having my little joke. Are you okay to drive?"

Marc scowled. "Yes, I am able to drive. I'm counting this your one-up-mans-ship. Consider this is your only warning that you're in my sights."

The crates of cocaine filled just Antonio's truck and they were on their way in less than half an hour. The weight of the cocaine was about 250 kilograms. On the road back, they were able to increase their speed due to to much less load weight.

With Homs receding in their rear mirror, Marc spoke. "So, what have we learned that will allow us to tank this operation?"

"Well," Peg responded. "Repeated air strikes would certainly disrupt this path. We'd need to notify the armed forces here in Syria to respond on short notice. We'd need to have spotters in both Italy and in Latakia. The one in Italy would have to be full time. Our man in Latakia should be in place a few days plus or minus, the expected arrival of the freighter. I don't like this one. Too much collateral damage. We could sink either ship, the American based one or the one with Lebanese registry, using a submarine, but again, too much collateral damage. We could have either ship boarded and the cargo confiscated. This brings up two other problems, Lebanon would consider it an act of war, and the other would be the CIA interfering in American businesses which is a no-no. That's about all."

"I noticed you didn't add having the Italian AISEI descending on the freighter once it's back in Italy." Marc said.

"No, if we set the AISEI on them that close to home base, Luigi would immediately jump to the conclusion that there was a leak in his organization. It wouldn't be that much of a leap that he had no problem before we showed up." Peg replied. "I hate the idea of that much cocaine getting into the American market, but we don't have a good enough plan yet. I think Peter needs to contact Sam Bear at the ATF and interrupt the shipment back in New Jersey. We can get the freighter name and number to Sam, so it would seem to be that the cocaine was caught on a random inspection."

"I like that one. It would intercept a load of arms and ammunition too." Marc replied. "It wouldn't make that big of a difference to the American Mafia. They would have factored in an occasionally loose of a shipment. They'll just find another ship and port of departure. What I like best is that there'd be nothing to tie it back to us. Gives us more time to put a plan in place."

"Well, it's a start of a plan." Peg said. "I'll call Peter. It's middle of the night there so I'll call him at home. His wife won't like it but it's kind of necessary."

Peg talked for half an hour to Peter. When she disconnected the call, she said, "Okay that's in the works. Want something to eat?"

Peg pulled a couple sandwiches from the box and then a bottle of Chianti.

"Wow!" Marc exclaimed. "I'm really hungry. What a way to travel."

Other than commenting on the quality for the food, they made the return to Latakia in silence.

Chapter 19

In Route to Molo Audace

With the drivers and the ship's crew working together, the cocaine was quickly loaded. There were several false compartments throughout the ship so it looked as if the ship was returning empty.

"Antonio," Marc asked. Won't the port inspectors get suspicious that there is no cargo?"

"No," Antonio replied. We'll make a stop in Dubrovnik and pick up a load of antique furniture. Both the cocaine and furniture will be loaded on the next leg going back to the States. The inspection at Molo Audace will be minimal because we pay the agent enough to not do a thorough check. In the States, it's handled much the same way. But that's our American cousin's problem."

"let's get on board. Dinner will be in two hours. Get some rest. I will call Luigi and let him know it was another successful trip."

Dinner was finished. Not talking business during meals seemed the rule here as well as at Villa de Falco. The steward had cleared away the dishes and at Antonio's direction, placed a goblet of Armagnac in front of each.

"Here's to another successful run," Antonio toasted. "Luigi was pleased."

"Do you often have problems," asked Peg.

"If it's a larger bandit group, we have had to shoot our way through." Antonio replied.

"What's different between the group we encountered and others? Marc asked.

"You need to understand we are not alone in wanting cocaine. The coast where we enter Syria is only about 125 kilometers long and Latakia is the only port. There is more or less a gentleman's agreement that we do not interfere with others. Other gun runners don't care who brings the cocaine. The larger bandit gangs want arms too. They don't compete directly with ISIS. They need arms to control their areas of Syria."

"How about using smaller craft that can land on the beaches?" Marc continued.

"Beach landings would not be necessary. There are several villages along the coast. They people there are fishermen and although the all have small piers, they're too small for a freighter. The logistics are just against it. Unloading the arms at sea would be tricky. Not to mention, a fleet of small boats would be required to get a fast unloading and where would those craft stay until the next shipment."

"Gotcha." Marc replied. "Thanks for the tutorial. This helping us a lot to see if expanding the operation is viable."

The rest of the voyage was low keyed. They read, played cards and answered Antonio's questions about the different cities in the States. Antonio called Luigi when they were about half a day out.

Chapter 20

Molo Audace

Friuli-Venezia Giulia, I*taly*

As the ship pulled to the dock, they could see the other freighter that would carry the cocaine and antique furniture on the next leg. Luigi was waiting at the foot of the gangway when it touched down. He seemed pleased to see them. He was not his usual calm and collected self.

"Bene tornato!" "welcome back!" He exclaimed. "Antonio has kept me apprised of your successful trip. He will supervise the transfer of the cargo and meet us back at the villa. We will have a late lunch and after that you can tell me are your thoughts of our operation are.

The handed off their bags to the driver and settle into the limousine. Peg took note of how close Luigi sat to Marc and that he rested his hand on Marc's thigh. When Luigi looked away, she gave Marc a long wink. He smiled in response. The trip back was filled with small talk. Luigi seem to not wanting to talk more about past events. He ignored Peg and was totally wrapped up in Marc. She didn't try to jump in, and just spent the ride looking at the passing scenery.

Chapter 21

Villa de Falco

Friuli-Venezia Giulia, *Italy*

Lunch was rainbow trout with wild dandelion greens paired with a smooth Sancerre. As usual, there was no business talk until after the meal. When the meal was finished, Carlo cleared the table and served coffee.

"Tell me what you thought of the operation?" Luigi asked.

"Everything seemed to go smoothly except for the bandit collecting a toll for use of the road." Marc responded.

"If we decide to expand the operation, there will be a need to double the number of truck or make two trips to Homs." Peg added.

"I will consider the trade-offs." Luigi replied. "Right now, the vessel moves off the pier to allow other ships to dock and then comes back to pick up Antonio. The port is not that busy and the docking fee is minimal. Antonio can investigate the logistics of keeping our vessel docked for two days."

As if Antonio had been summoned, he walked up the stairs to the patio. "I heard what you were talking about and have taken note of what you want. I will talk to the port officials the next trip to Latakia." Antonia said.

"When is the next shipment of arms due?" Peg asked.

"It would be in about two weeks." Luigi responded.

"How is that possible?" Asked Peg. "It takes over two weeks for the ship leaving here to get to the States."

"we have a second ship standing by in case we have an extra shipment of arms." Luigi responded. "The flow of arms is erratic, so it pays to have another ship on call."

"I think I see a possible way to increase the number of arms to be shipped. We could possibly get several Families, in the States, to join us for a share in the cocaine." Marc said.

If you can make that work, I have no problem arranging for another ship on this end." Luigi said.

"We'd like to go on at least one more trip, if it's okay with you." Marc asked.

"That will not be an issue." Luigi replied as he scooted his chair back from the table and stood up. Why don't you refresh your selves and have a rest? Cocktails will be served in the great room at seven."

Peg and Marc got up from the table and followed Luigi into the house. The foursome climbed the stairs and went to their respective rooms.

Fifteen minutes later, the was a soft rap on Peg's door. She quickly opened it a let Marc enter. "I was afraid that was Antonio at my door." Peg said.

Marc laughed and quietly closed the door. "I guess he's tired from supervising the transfer of the cocaine and furniture to the other vessel. He surely will be perked up by cocktail time and will be sitting next to you."

"I'm not that attracted to him, but I going to allow him to get close so I can learn more about the total operation not just this last leg that we joined." Peg added. "He likes to ramble on, so I have to listen to a lot of crap about himself, just to learn something solid."

"Have you given an update to Peter and our Italian cousins?" Marc asked.

"Yes, we went through the different options and basically everyone agrees that and air strike on the caravan would be too much collateral damage. We talked at length about intercepting any of the shipment would make us out to be international pirates. Everyone likes confiscating the shipment when it reaches the States. That could be hit or miss. What they need from us is the ship's name and registration number." Peg detailed.

"yeah," Marc remarked. "That will only good for one or two times before Luigi and the American Mafia came to the same conclusion that there is a mole in the operation and that could lead to looking at us more closely."

"Okay, you're right. Let's only do it once so it looks as if the inspectors caught the cocaine shipment by chance." Peg said. "Did you by chance notice the ship's name and registration on the one going to the States."

"No," Marc replied. "we'll have to wait for the next shipment."

"Maybe not," Peg said. "I bet Luigi has all that information somewhere in his study. Next time you and Luigi have a get together, I'll search his study."

"He probably keeps his study locked," Marc added.

"Not to worry." Peg responded. "I have my manicure set."

Peg's manicure set was indeed a manicure set but in the lining was a sophisticate lock pic set.

"Let me borrow your eye glasses so I can get a photo of anything that I find." Peg added.

"I'm going back to my room and get some rest." Marc said. "See you at seven."

At quarter to seven, Marc knocked on Peg's door. She was wearing another new dress cut very provocable.

Marc chuckled. "I see that you are ready win over Antonio."

"That won't be hard." Peg responded.

"Shall we?" Marc cocked his arm for Peg to take.

They made their way down the staircase and to the great room. Luigi and Antonio were already there and Peg's and Marc's drinks were poured.

"Ah, you're getting use to us. Thank you." Marc said.

"I want your stay to be a rememberable experience." Luigi said looking directly into Marc's eyes.

"So far it's been a pleasant experience." Marc returned Luigi gaze.

"It certainly has." Peg added.

"I'm going to make sure you have a pleasant stay too." Antonio added taking Peg's arm and leading her to the love seat.

Peg smiled at him as he sat beside her. "Thank you, Antonio. I'd like to get to know you better."

Antonio beamed and for a change he didn't seem to find the words to respond.

Peg gave a small laugh and looked directly into his eyes. She didn't think his smile could get any bigger but it did.

Marc and Luigi were looking at the exchange. They looked at each other and smiled.

Antonio wanted them to talk more about the big cities in the States, which they did, but Marc and Peg wanted to know more about the Villa Falco and the surrounding area.

Luigi laughed at the mixed exchange. "I need to inspect the different sublets of land tomorrow. I will do it on horseback. Would you like to join me?"

Peg and Marc responded "yes" at the same time.

Luigi turned to Antonio. "You're welcome to join us Antonio."

Antonio looked at Peg and then back to Luigi. "Yes, I'd like that very much."

Carlo appeared at the door to announce that dinner was ready. They followed Luigi into the dining room.

Dinner was duck L'Orange with pureed butternut squash followed with a green salad. It was complemented with a Chianti with the duck and crisp pinot grigio with the salad. Desert was peach cobbler.

Marc sat back. "You certainly have a wonderful chef. Please give out complements to her or him."

"Nicol has been with Family way before my time. My greatest fear is that he will retire. He is eighty. I'm not sure he could be replaced." Luigi answered. "Shall we retire to the great room for some Armagnac?"

Later, Marc and Luigi retired to Luigi's bedroom. Peg and Antonio talked for an anther hour.

Peg stifle a fake yawn and said: "I'm sorry, Antonio, but I need to go to my room. I'm really tired."

Antonio looked disappointed. "I would have like to spent more time with you, but let me escort you to your room."

"Thanks," Peg replied.

At Peg's door, Antonio took her hand and kissed her palm for a few seconds. He released her hand and said: "Buona notte. I'll see you at breakfast."

At midnight, Peg eased her door open and looked both ways down the hallway. Most of the lights were turned off. She was dressed all in black including softs soled shoes. Making her way to Luigi's study, she tried the door but it was locked. She took out her "nail case" and kneeling, she had the door open in five seconds. She went immediately to the desk and went through the drawers. Find nothing of import, she turned to the filing cabinet. It was locked but it was a simple lock and she was in it one second. She found agreements with ISIS and the American Mafia. Each had terms of set amounts of arms and cocaine. The agreement with ISIS was straight forward, for "x" number of arms for "x" number kilos of cocaine. The agreement with the American Mafia, named the Family. That was a find, as to date the ATF didn't know which Family was running the operation in the States. Taking out Marc's glasses, she took photos the two agreements. Locking the filing cabinet and the study door, she made her way back to her room.

At seven in the morning, Marc knocked on her door. "Morning Magdalena, how did you sleep?"

"Well," she responded. "What there was of it. Let's go get some coffee and I'll tell what I found last night." Whispering, she told him what she had found and that she had sent the photos on to Langley.

"Good work, Marc whispered just before they entered the dining room.

They found Luigi and Antonio seated at the table with just coffee.

"Good morning," Luigi greeted. "I hope you slept well."

"Yes. I did," Peg and Marc said in unison.

"Breakfast is ready." Luigi said. Motioning with his hand to the sideboard.

There was a spread of scrambled eggs, bacon, sausage, pancakes, fruit and an urn of coffee.

"Take what pleases you. We are going to have a full day of riding. Nicol has packed a basket for our lunch and a blanket. There are several spots that would be good for a picnic."

Peg and Marc filled their plates and sat at the table and waited for Luigi and Antonio to do the same.

When the two were seated, Marc asked: "What's on the agenda for today?"

"Mostly just checking on the health of the farm land and inspecting the houses, barns and storage buildings to see if they need repair. Also, to check on the storage bins to see if the harvest is reasonable. Some of the tenants take a portion of the produce to sell on the side. They are paid a good salary, but it's just the nature of the beast to want more."

"I have Levies and gym shoes. Will that be sufficient for the ride?" asked Peg.

"Same here." Marc echoed.

"Yes, but boots would have been better. Just watch where you step when we are a round the farm animals. We'll meet at the stables in a half hour."

Leaving the stables, they made their way down a dirt road. Conversation was mostly small talk; Marc and Peg asking the names of crops and trees. They rode for half an hour before turning off the road to reach the first plot. Luigi greeted each tenant and the workers by name; asking about their Families. His inspection of the storage bins was made in an apologetic manner, but he was thorough. They visited four more plots before stopping for lunch around two in the afternoon.

They stopped in a wooded glen next to a small stream. Lunch was a surprise: fois gras, cheese, fruit and a bottle of Chianti. Marc and Peg were amazed to see crystal goblets, wrapped in towels, for the wine.

"I hope you never lose Nicol." Peg exclaimed. "This is the best!"

Luigi laughed. "It will be a sad day when he leaves, but we can't halt time."

"I have a question," Marc said. "Your land, excuse me, the Families land is extensive but at least half is stands of trees and open pasture. Couldn't you make better use of the land by doing more farming?"

"Certainly," Luigi responded. "The answer is simple. I'm very fond of hunting with the falcons so I'm indulging my selfish side."

Marc laughed. "I see your point and if it were up to me, I'd do the same."

They loaded up the remains of their lunch and rode on. They visited four more tenants and arrive back at the stables at five. Leaving the horses to the stable hands, they walked back to the villa.

"Thank you, Luigi, that was a pleasant experience." Peg said.

"You are more than welcome," Luigi responded.

They entered the villa and climbed the stairs to their rooms. Before they parted, Luigi said: "Refresh and rest yourselves. Cocktails will be at seven."

Dinner that evening was roast pork with apple sauce, wild greens, roasted potatoes. The wine was another Sancerre. Desert was mixed berries in heavy cream.

Over Armagnac they discussed options for increasing the flow of arms and cocaine.

Luigi said after reviewing several scenarios, "I like the increase in arms shipments and In upping of the number of ships. Do you think your Family will go along with joining with other American Families?"

"We will see," Marc responded. "I've already presented the plan to our Don. He'll probably take some time to get back to us. This is a major step. He will want to mull it over. Then he will choose the Families he thinks will agree to the deal.

Later in the evening, Luigi stood. Saying good night to Peg and Antonio, he took Marc's hand to lead him upstairs.

Antonio moved closer to Peg and leaned in for a kiss. Peg responded and their kiss became more passionate.

"Will you spend the night with me?" Antonio pleaded.

"No," Peg paused.

Antonio's smile dropped.

Peg gave a small laugh. "No," she repeated. "But I will spend some time with you in my room. I just prefer to have the majority of the night in my bed--alone."

Antonio smiled and shrugged. Taking her hand, he led up the stairs.

The next morning after breakfast, Luigi turned to Peg and asked if she would like to try her hand at falconry. She quickly replied yes.

"May I try it again," asked Marc.

"Certainly," Luigi answered. "Dinner is on you two, so we'll see how good you are. We are going further out this time so we'll take horses."

"You'll need more rugged clothing so change and meet us at the stable in half an hour. The beaters have already left and will meet us about four kilometer out."

They rode to the falconry where two men were waiting with the falcons on their arms. Luigi directed them to provide padded sleeves to Peg and Marc. "We will walk the horses to allow the birds to get adjusted to the motion and then pick up some speed in about a kilometer."

The men handed off the birds to Peg and Marc. Luigi was unsure if Peg could carry the falcon on her arm for any period of time, but her martial arts training more than prepared her.

They arrived at a small stand of trees and bushes where the beaters were waiting.

"Marc," Luigi said. "Show Magdalena how to loft the birds."

Marc un-hooded his falcon and moved his arm up. The bird flew to the top of a tree. Peg copied him and her falcon landed on a nearby tree.

"Andiamo," Luigi called to the beaters. They proceed into the trees whacking their poles into the brush. Quickly, they could hear movement of some type animal through the foliage.

The falcons lifted off and flew to the other side of the grove. From their vantage point, they could see the falcons hovering and then diving toward the ground. The foursome rode around the trees that the birds had each caught two large hares.

"Bene!" Antonio exclaimed. "We have dinner!"

Marc chuckled and Peg could not stop laughing at Antonio's enthusiasm.

The beaters quickly gutted the hares and fed the entrails to the falcons. After they had eaten, the beaters were bringing the birds back to Marc and Peg when Luigi interrupted. "Let's exchange arm padding and Antonio and I will try our luck."

They walked the horses across a small meadow to another stand of trees. The beaters took their positions as Luigi and Antonio lofted their birds to the tree tops. Luigi called to the beaters and they moved into trees and brush. Soon, there was a repeat of animal movement under the trees. The falcons flew to the far side of the grove and hovered before diving to the ground. They rode around the grove to see that the birds had taken down two roe deer.

This time, Peg and Marc both shouted: "Bene!"

The beaters repeated the gutting and feeding the falcons. It was a slower process as the falcons had already sated their hunger. They left the rest of the entrails for other animals. Llowering their arms, the falcons leapt up to the padded arms. Other beaters, gather the carcasses and headed back to the villa.

"Let's ride out for a while. I'd like to check on another farm while we're out in this direction." Luigi said.

They rode for another half hour and arrived at a small farm. Luigi rode up to the farm house and called out to the residents. An older couple came out and Luigi spoke to them for a while, the mounted his horse and rode back to the trio. "Let's ride back to the villa. By the time we clean up, lunch should be ready. I believe it's going to be roast hare."

The rode at a faster pace. Reaching the stables, they turned the horses over to the stable hands and walked to the villa.

"Get cleaned up," Luigi said. "Lunch will be on the patio in an hour."

They went to their respected rooms. Half an hour later, Marc knocked softly on Peg's door. She quickly opened the door and motioned him in.

"Let's go out on the balcony." Peg said softly.

"Any more thoughts on terminating this operation?" Marc asked.

"Yes, I have," Peg responded. "How about we have our Italian friends in the AISE stage a raid when the ship gets back with its load of cocaine. They could arrest everyone at the dock and then come to the villa an arrest Luigi."

"That' a possibility," Marc replied. I think we should pass this idea by Alfred and Dominico and get their take on this plan. We'd have to be positive on making the charges stick or this would only result in a short delay."

"Don Giovanni is still in prison, so some type charge is making him serve a sentence. Let's try to work it in to the conversation over lunch." Marc said. "Shall we go down for lunch?"

Luigi and Antonio were seated and rose as Peg and Marc came out to the patio. As Luigi had predicted, lunch as roast hare. It was served with garden vegetables and paired with a dry Chablis. Dessert was a choice of several flavors of gelato.

After coffee was served, Peg turned to Luigi and asked: "How long will you be serving as head of the Family until Don Giovanni is released?"

"He won't be released. He's in for murder. I will head the Family until he passes or until he decides to replace me." Luigi responded.

"That's amazing," Marc injected. "He puts a lot of faith in you."

"No really." Luigi replied. "If I don't follow his directions, he would back one of the other lieutenants to replace me. I couldn't resist as The Family does whatever he dictates."

"Is there a chance that he will die in Prison?" asked Peg.

"Yes, that's a possibility," Luigi answered. "But he's only in his sixties and in good health."

"And, who would replace you if you fall out of favor with him?" Marc asked.

"There are three other lieutenants. The one most likely to replace me would be Francisco Ricci. Luigi said. "They have villas in the surrounding area. They're involved in several ventures to bring money to the Family—robbery, ransom, and protection. Their income does not compare to mine and they're jealous of my operation."

"Sounds like you have to be vigilant," Marc remarked.

"Not really," Luigi replied. "I keep an eye on them, but it will remain status quo until Don Giovanni says otherwise."

The next two weeks passed quickly. They flew the falcons once more but there was plenty of fresh game in the freezer so there was no need. They rode horseback several times—not to inspect farms but to just enjoy the scenery. Marc and Peg gave two more martial arts demonstrations. This time, they spent time sparring with some of the soldiers, including Antonio. He asked Peg to teach him the move she used taking down the Gambini soldier in Venice. He was a good study and she complemented his style, which caused him to puff up and smile broadly.

Prior to their sailing, Peg had presented their idea on staging a raid when they returned with the next load of heroine. Alfredo said he'd pass it by his superiors and get back to them. It was the night before leaving for Syria before they got an answer.

On the way to dinner, Peg whispered to Marc that she had a response and would tell him that evening.

Dinner that evening was pheasant with wild asparagus paired with a robust Chianti. Desert was chocolate cake and coffee.

"I'm not sure I can continue this diet," Peg remarked. "My clothes seem to be fitting more tightly. I'm going to work it off while we are at sea. I wouldn't insult Nicol by refusing to eat anything he prepares." The three men laughed.

They all pushed back from the table and filed into the great room for Armagnac and for Luigi his nightly cigar.

"We have not seen the ship that brings the arms to your port." Said Marc. "We'd like to see how the arms are hidden to see it's possible to hide an increase."

"We don't unpack the crates. We load them on the other ship as they are. It saves time. The weapons and ammunition are at the bottom of the crates that have boxes of canned food." Antonio interjected. "The food is a bonus for ISIS."

"Sounds good, but we'd like to see if an increase would get by inspection." Marc replied.

"No problem." Antonio replied. "I would be leaving soon to supervise the transfer. You or the both of you are welcome to come with me."

Peg said: "I'll go. Pietro can stay here and keep Luigi company."

"It's going to be cool, so grab a jacket and meet me at the front steps." Antonio said.

Peg nodded and left the room. Getting her jacket, she found Antonio in his sports car. The passenger door was open. She slid in to the seat and they roared off.

Back in the great room Marc and Luigi were chatting. "Can you tell me more about your Families structure?" Marc asked. "If you'll pardon me, it seems as though you are not really in charge. Don Giovanni could redirect your operation on a whim."

"You are correct." Luigi responded. "Don Giovanni started these arms for heroin trade before he went to prison. I was working closely with him, so I was a natural choice to keep it running, but my position as second-in-command is at his whim."

"How long is he in for?" Marc asked.

"Our country usually doesn't hand out life sentences, but it came out in the trial, that he had directed multiple hits. Ergo the life sentence." Luigi responded. "I report to him weekly and go over in detail the profit from the arms trade and how our share of the cocaine is distributed. He makes changes that he feels would be better for the

Family, so you see I'm not really in charge. He has allowed me to make busines investments that bring profits and stand up to government inspection. This was my idea as a backup for the Family if a majority of our operations were to be shut down. The investments are doing very well."

"That's very good." Marc responded. "Our family does the same. It's a good insurance plan."

"How about you?" Marc asked. "You say you're bi-sexual so does that mean you will wed some time?"

"I guess," Luigi replied. "My mother is constantly on me to get married so she will have grand-children. She knows about me being bi-sexual but she's sure that it's just a phase. I have two brothers and a sister who have children so I don't know why she picks on me."

"To be honest, I'm much more comfortable being gay than when I'm being bisexual. This is the usual response gay Italian man give when they are gay and want to have a family. Then, they have their boyfriends on the side. The wife knows but they just live with it so they can keep a family together."

"We have a similar problem in the States, but the wife doesn't know — she may suspect but the husbands are discreet with their liaisons."

"So, are you going to have permanent boyfriend some day?" Marc asked.

"Don Giovanni would not like it if I did. He's quite homophobic. This will continue until he dies or I'm no longer second-in-command. Why, are you applying for the position?"

Marc laughed. "I'm afraid not. I have a lot of responsibilities back in the States. There is no one special, just Family busines. It's tempting but I'm not sure I could make the change."

"Well, think about it. The position won't open unless the two things occur that I told you about. Are you ready to retire?" Luigi asked.

"Sure," Marc replied.

They made their way up the stairs to Luigi's room.

A round midnight, Marc went to his own room. He tapped lightly on Peg's door but got no response. He listened at Antonio's door but could not hear any sounds. Going back to his room, he sat up reading, knowing Peg would tap on his door when she returned.

At the stroke of 1 AM, there was a soft knock on Marc's door. He opened the door and Peg slipped in. "That was an interesting experience. They do a very good job of hiding the arms and ammunitions. If I were a inspector, I'd let the shipment pass."

"On my response from Alfredo: he doesn't think a raid on the ship here would be of much benefit. He believes the captain and crew would take responsibly for the cargo as the Family would have promised that they would take care of their families in this eventuality. Their sentences would be around five years. We are back to zero. Maybe this next trip will reveal something we can use. I'm for bed. Tomorrow comes early. 'Night."

"Good night." Marc replied as he opened the door for Peg.

Chapter 22

Molo Audace

Friuli-Venezia Giulia, *Italy*

Next Morning

Antonio ha left earlier to supervise the transfer of the arms and food product to the other ship. Luigi had insisted that he drive Marc and Peg to the ship and see them off. When they arrived, the last pallet was descending on to the Syria bound ship. Antonio wave to them from the upper deck motioning them to come aboard. Marc and Peg retrieved their hand bags from the truck of Luigi's car and took them to the bottom of the gangplank.

Luigi walk over with them. "Have a good trip and stay safe," he said. He shook Peg's hand but pulled Marc into an embrace. "I'll miss you."

Marc answered: "I'll miss you too. Take care of yourself."

Marc and Peg went up the gangplank and made their way to the staterooms.

Peg stopped at Marc's door. "Looks as if things are getting serious between you two."

"He is really a nice person." Marc responded. "I don't think he's into his position of second-in-command. It sems to me that, if he had a choice, he like a less complicated life."

"Just watch yourself, okay? Peg replied. "We are going to destroy his operation so he'll be looking at you a lot differently."

"I know," Marc answered. "I wish could stop the whole arms for cocaine operation and get him out of the fallout."

"That's nice, but get your head out of your ass and stick to business!" Peg said raising her voice on the last part.

"You are right of course; I will stick to business." Marc said softly.

Peg patted him on the side of his face and kissed his cheek. She turned away and went to her stateroom.

The ship stared to move and they went out to the deck. Luigi was still standing there. Seeing them, he waved. Marc waved in response. Peg just lifted her arm.

Chapter 23

At Sea

The threesome agreed. This part of the trip was boring. They read, played cards or monopoly, watched movies and slept. Conversation was mostly on the States—Antonio's favorite subject. Peg occasionally talked to Alfredo, there Italian contact and to Peter the boss back at Langley. She did not have much to report—just that they had not come up with a plan to disrupt the flow of arms and cocaine.

One evening, Peg went out on the deck to get some fresh air and found Marc staring off into space. "Penny for your thoughts," she asked.

"I'm not sure they are worth that much," he replied. "I'm trying to work out a plan to disrupt this whole operation. I keep coming up with zero. And to tell the truth, my mind turns back to Luigi. I'd like some way to not have to put him at risk. I don't think we'll come up with a way with having the lot arrested. That's Alfredo's and Domenico's problem, but I don't see Luigi as a criminal."

"Do you include Antonio in that scenario?" Peg asked.

"No, I don't. He seems to like what he's doing. What do you think? He asked.

"I agree with you about Antonio, but I'm not sure about Luigi. He's a grown person. He's second-in-command. He knows what he's doing. How can you not believe he's fully aware of his involvement?" Asked Peg.

"You are right of course. To be honest, I've developed strong feeling for him. I got your warning and I'll be standing firm when this game plays out." Marc sighed. "I think I'll go to my cabin and read. See you later, Maggi."

"See you later, Pietro. I'm going to the lounge to have an intelligent conversation with Antonio."

When Peg entered the lounge, she found Antonio play a game on the computer. "Hey Antonio, I see you're keeping busy."

"I'm so bored. I'm passing time doing no-brainer games." He responded. "Do you want to play cards or a board game?"

"No, let's talk about you. I've pretty much told you my life's story but I don't know much about you." Peg said.

"I've not got much to tell. I come from a poor family. But not poor any more. I make a good salary so I send them money every month. "I started working the streets when I was fifteen — stealing and picking pockets. Picking pockets was an education.

|I was not very good at first, so I would just run away. I was very fast. As I got better, the marks never knew they were missing their wallets."

"There was this guy. Very well dressed. Looked like an easy mark. He was fast — grabbed my wrist and nearly broke it. He said; you're good. Want to come to work for me?" Antonio said. "Doing what?"

"Just running errands at first. Making collections when you're older and then selling dope." He replied. "Interested?"

"How much," Antonio asked.

"One hundred seventy thousand Lira a week to start. If you work out, that will go up." The man replied.

"Thus started my life of crime. I've looked back and never regrated my decision."

"How about your family? Did they care about the direction your life was taking?" Peg asked.

"No, I was sharing my take from my street work, so they were happy to get more."

"How many in your family? Peg asked.

"Six," he replied. Father, Mother and three sisters. The sisters are all married off now, and my parents are living well."

"And you, have you every married?" Peg said.

"Nope, not even close. I like my single life and I don't care about kids, so I'm a happy guy." Antonio answered.

"Are you hungry? I can tell the steward to start lunch." Antonio said.

"Sure," she responded. "I'll go get Pietro." Peg took the ladder at the end of the lounge and went down to the next deck. She knocked on Marc's door. There was no answer so she knocked again louder and heard a muffled: "Coming."

Marc opened his door to see Peg smiling at him.
"Getting some shut eye?" She asked.

"Not really,' Marc relied. "I was reading and fell asleep siting up. What's up?"

"Lunch is soon. Can I come in?"

"Sure." Marc opened the door wider.

Peg gave him a run-down on her conversation with Antonio.

"Huh," Marc grunted. "So, on one hand we have a profession criminal, Antonio, and on the other we have a question mark, Luigi."

"You don't think Luigi is a criminal?" She asked.

"The jury's out on that. I'd like to think Luigi is a victim of circumstance." Marc answered. "We'll just have to wait and see. Let's go to lunch."

Marc and Peg entered the lounge to see the steward setting out place settings.

Lunch will be in half an hour." Antonio said. "Would anyone like a cocktail?"

"Sure," Marc replied. I'll have scotch neat."

"I'll have the same," Peg added.

"That's three," Antonio said turning to the bar.

Lunch was steamed halibut, mashed potatoes, and green beans pair with a smooth Sancerre. They all turned down dessert, claiming weight gains.

Each day passed much the same until they reached Latakia.

Chapter 24

Port of Latakia, Syria

They arrive at Latakia in late morning. Unloading the arms crates took over two hours as they stopped for lunch. That meant, they would not get to Homs until after dark. They drove slowly on the dirt road due to the conditions. They picked-up speed when they reached the paved road, but still had to dodge the pot holes. Two hours later, the caravan came to a halt. The road was bordered by thick brush on each side of the road. Peg and Marc were in the last truck. They both got out.

"You stay here and I'll go see what's going on." Marc said

He walked up to the lead truck to find Antonio and his driver in a conversation with four men. They were armed and pointing the rifles at them. The driver was speaking Arab. Marc could only understand Antonio' side of the conversation.

"Chiedere loro quanto passare?" "Ask them how much to pass?" Antonio asked.

The driver turned to the four men. "As'alhum kam yumar?"

"Sanakhudh shahinatan wahidatan lilsamah lak bialmururi." "We will take one truck to allow you to pass." The oldest of the men replied.

The driver translated for Antonio:" Prenderemo un camion per farti passare." "We will take one truck to allow you to pass."

Marc asked: "Are you going to let them have a truck?"

"Don't have much choice," Antonio responded. "They've got the drop on us. I thought it was just a fee to use their road so we didn't come out armed. Dite loro che sarà come si dice. Tell them it will be as they say." He directed the driver.

"Sayakun kama taqul." "It is as you say." The driver waved them to the first truck.

Three men got in the truck, the fourth stood on the running board as they drove to a side road and disappeared.

"Shit!" Exclaimed Antonio. "That's going to cost us. We'll triple up on the next two trucks. Shit! We've lost our arms too. Let's get going."

Marc ran back to his truck to find Peg missing. He could see signs of a struggle and there was a part of Peg's shirt, next to the truck. "Antonio, wait!" He yelled.

Antonio ran back to Marc's truck. "What?" He asked.

"Maggi is gone." He shouted. "They must have gone this way," as he started on a trail in a break it the brush. Fifty feet in, the trail split three ways. "Crap," he exclaimed. "I'm seeing nothing but goat tracks and foot prints. Wait," he said. Starting on the trail to the right. "Here is a piece of Maggi's shirt. Smart girl."

Antonio yelled for his driver to join them.

They walked for about four miles. Each time, the trail split, they found a piece of Peg's shirt. Coming up to a rise, they smell smoke and advanced in a crouch. Looking down to a small flat area, they saw three mud-brick buildings. Smoke was coming from the largest building. There was a small building off to the side with a man standing guard. There was only a small window in the back that was barred.

"It will be dark soon so let's wait before we do anything." Marc whispered. "If something else happens, we'll play it by ear."

Antonio whispered: "I'm not familiar with term 'play it by ear'. What does that mean?"

Marc chuckled. "It means we make a decision on what to do as the event presents itself."

"I like that", Antonio said. I have a new American saying. Play it by ear."

They laid down, not speaking as the light faded. Night arrived. The only illumination were the stars and a half moon. The odor of cooking meat drifted up the slope to them.

"Stay here until I've taken down the guard by the small building, and if Maggi is there, I'll release her. I will wave to you when it's time to join me."

Marc circled around until he could get to the back side of the small building. He moved slowly trying not to make any sound. Reaching the window, he scratched on the bars. There was movement inside and a shape came to the window. "Peg is that you?" He whispered.

"Marc?" she spoke softly.

"Yeah. Are you hurt?"

"No," she answered. "But my hands are tied."

"No problem. Give me a few minutes and I'll have you out of there."

Marc slowly made his way around the building. Lying down, he looked around the corner. The guard was facing the bigger building at an angle that would reveal Marc if he advanced on the guard. Drawing back, he got to his feet and moved around the building until he was at the corner behind the guard. Again, he laid down and looked around the corner. The guard's gaze was fixed on the larger building, probably anticipating his dinner. The odor of the cooking meat was strong. Marc crept up behind him and grabbed him in a choke hold. The guard tried to call out but only gasps came out. Slowly, he stopped struggling and his body went limp. Marc laid him down and pulled him away from the door. Addressing the door, he found just a simple latch. He opened the door slowly to avoid any squeaks. When the opening was wide enough, Peg stepped out. She lifted her hands to Marc. He took his boot knife out and slashing her bindings.

"Thanks. What took you so long to get here." She whispered.

"Just be glade I'm here." He waved his arms and Antonio and the driver came down the slope.

Antonio tried to hug Peg but she pushed him away. He had retrieved her automatic rifle from their truck and handed it to her. She whispered: "Thanks."

Marc motioned them all to approach the main building. Standing in front of the door, he mimed kicking the doo open. He got a nod from the other three. He gave a solid kick and the door swung open and slammed against the inside wall. They all rush in with their rifle pointed at the men inside.

There were five men and two women in the room. The interior was dirt floor covered with several rugs. Both of the women screamed. One in the process of handing a bowl of food to the eldest of the men, dropped the bowl in his lap. He screamed as the hot food soaked into his groin. The other four men raised their hands. The rifles they'd use to hijack the truck were leaning against the wall. One of the me started to reach for a rifle. The driver swung his firearm to that man and said: "La." "Do not."

The eldest said: "Min fadlik la tudhina. naetadhir ean 'akhadh shahinatuk." "Please do not harm us. We apologize for taking your truck."

Antonio asked the driver. "Cosa ha detto?" "What did he say?"

Ha chiesto di non far loro del male e si è dispiaciuto per aver rubato il camion." "He asked not to harm them and he was sorry for stealing the truck."

Antonio took out his side arm and shot him in the forehead.

"Shit!" Peg yelled. "Why the fuck did you do that?"

"They need to be taught a lesson or they will just do it again." Antonio answered.

Peg looked disgusted. "You didn't have to kill him. You could have shot him in the leg."

Antonio said nothing, shrugging his shoulders.

"Enough! Marc exclaimed. Antonio tell your diver to collect their rifles and let's' get out of here."

"Prendi i fucili." "Get the rifles." The drive took the rifles and backed out of the door.

The men were silent but sullen. The women were wailing.

Marc and Antonio exited, leaving Peg facing the room. "I know you can't understand me, but I am very sorry." She turned and left the room.

They all met at the truck and Marc open the driver's door and found the keys still in the ignition. Antonio told the driver to get into the back of the truck. He got into the driver's position. Marc and Peg walked around the truck and Marc open the door and motion Peg in, but she shook her head and motioned Marc to sit next to Antonio.

Thirty minutes later they were at the caravan. Antonio took his position at the head. Marc and Peg walked back to their truck. As the pasted each, Marc said: "Va bene." "It's good."

They were several hours late for the planned time to arrive at Homs. Speaking through his driver, Antonio recounted what caused the delay. When he got to the part where he shot one of the men, they replied back as through he'd taken the right action.

Marc and Peg were listening to the exchange. Although Peg did not under stand all that was said, caught the approval of Antonio shooting the man.

She snorted and turn away in anger.

They took part in sampling the heroin again but not as much as last time. When the transfer of arms for heroin was completed, they got back in their truck and move out for the return to Latakia. Peg was silent.

"Penny for your thoughts." Marc asked.

"I'm not sure they are worth that much," she responded. "I'm really pissed. Antonio did not have to kill that guy."

"You're right Peg O'my heart. But you realize, Antonio has been a criminal all his life. I'm sure he's killed before."

"I'm going to have to calm down and get back in his good graces or I'm going to blow this operation." She replied. "I'll let him apologize and tell him, I understand. At the same time, I'll be biting my tongue. Oh, the things I do for my country."

Marc laughed. "Down to business. Have you any ideas on disrupting this operation?"

"No," she replied. "Everything we've considered either involves collateral damage or it's only a short-term interruption." There is something we haven't considered. The government troops are just about to re-take Homs. This operation could die a natural death. Let's ask Luigi if he's come up with a plan for that contingency."

They rode mostly in silence back to Latakia. The cocaine was loaded quickly and they were on the way back to Italy.

Chapter 25

At Sea

Peg went to her cabin as soon as they boarded the ship. Antonio tried to talk to her, but she remained silent. When dinner was about to be served, Marc went to her cabin and knocked on her door.

"Who is it she called out."

"It's Pietro," Marc said.

"A moment," she responded. Slipping into a robe, she opened the door.

"You hungry?" Marc asked.

"No, I'm still upset over Antonio killing that guy. I wouldn't be able to hide it. I'm going to stay in my cabin and do some meditation. By morning, I should be able to put up a professional façade."

"Okay. Then I'll see you in the morning." Marc said.

"See ya," she replied closing her door.

Marc went to the lounge. Antonio had poured three Scotches — neat. "She's not coming to dinner?" He asked.

"No, she's tired and wants to go to bed early." Marc responded.

"I think she's pissed at me." He said.

"Maybe," Marc replied. "She'll get over it. She is not use to violence. We usually resolve difference inside our Family and outside the Family through negotiations."

They fell back into their routine reading, playing cards and games. Peg would retreat to her cabin for meditation frequently. Which seemed to help as she and Antonio were back go good terms.

They made one stop at Corfu, Greece to pick up crates of antique furniture.

Chapter 26

Molo Audace

Friuli-Venezia Giulia, I*taly*

They arrived at Molo Audace late morning. Luigi was waiting for them as their ship pulled into the dock. He stood at the bottom the of the gangplank. Marc led the trio down to the dock. Luigi immediately pull him into a long embrace. Peg, he lightly embraced and he shook Antonio's hand. "Antonio told me, over the satellite phone, that you've had a bit of excitement.' He said that all was worked out and the full shipment of arms was delivered."

"He also told me about Magdalena being upset over shooting the Arab. I agree with Magdalena. It was excessive. Antonio and I will work this out later. He will stay to supervise the transfer of cocaine and furniture."

They went to Luigi's sedan and climbed in. Marc was next to Luigi — Peg in the back seat. Luigi took the most direct route so they were back at the villa in half an hour. Luigi asked and received a detail account of the high-jacking. He congratulated Peg on her fortitude and cleverness in leaving a trail with pieces of shirt, and Marc on his skill in resolving the altercation.

Chapter 27

Villa Falco

Friuli-Venezia Giulia, *Italy*

"I'm sure you'll want to clean up. Lunch will be in half an hour. Luigi said.

"Looking forward to it," said Peg. "The cook, aboard the ship, sets a pretty good table, but he doesn't compare to Nicol's cooking."

Luigi laughed.

Lunch on the patio was roasted salmon served with garden vegetables and complemented with a smooth Pinot Noir. Desert was apple pie and coffee.

When they'd pushed back from the table, Luigi said: Let's go to the study and talk.

"You've had two trips now, each with different experiences. What are your thoughts on expanding the operation? Luigi asked.

"We think it can be done," Marc answered. "But I have a question or maybe two. ISIS is losing the battle in Homs. The government troops are more than two-thirds across the city. There might not be a place to deliver the arms in another two weeks. What's the contingency plan if the troops take the whole city?"

"ISIS is going to come up with an alternate place to take possession of the arms. Probably north to Aleppo," Luigi responded. "They still have a presence there."

"Can we look at a map please," asked Peg.

Luigi went to his map cabinet and pulled out a large map of Syria and spread in on his desk. He traced a path from Latakia up route M4 to M5; then directly into Aleppo. It's actually shorter than to Homs," he said.

"I guess, I have a third question," Marc said. "ISIS is losing the war. How much longer can your operation continue?"

"That's the question," Luigi replied. "They've already asked us to increase the shipments, so we'll continue until there's no longer a market. That could be months or even years. As long as there is profit to be made, Don Giovanni has directed me to continue. So, if you can increase the number of arms and ammunition and take care of a larger vessel, we'll take care of things on our end."

"I think we have a go then," Marc replied. "I'll tell the ones working this in our Family to plan on an increase. We'll work out the details when we get back to the States."

"You'll be leaving soon?" Luigi asked. He looked troubled.

"Yes," Peg said. "I'll talk to the States to see if there is anything else, they want us to do and if not, we'll leave in the morning. We would like to thank you for your hospitality. I speak for both of us. This has been more of a vacation than a work assignment."

"Yes, it has," added Marc.

"I'll see if Nicol can fix something special as a going-away dinner." Luigi remarked

Peg laughed. "I don't know how he can top what he's already prepared."

"Okay, now for some quiet time. I'll see you for cocktails as seven." Luigi said. "Marc, will you stay and talk to me for a few minutes."

"Sure," he responded.

Luigi folded up the map and put it away. He motioned Marc over to a pair of armchairs by the fireplace. "I'm going to miss you. I've become very fond of you. Have you given some thought to staying or returning?"

Marc sighed. "It's very tempting, but I'd lose my standing in the Family. You don't need a third hand to run your operation, so what would I do to earn my keep?"

"I haven dwelled much on my other involvements, but there is plenty to do in my legitimate businesses. I could use some help there."

"I'll promise you this: I'll give it some serious thought and you think about what I would do specifically, and we'll talk after I get home. Right now, Maggi and I are the point persons to expanding the operation. I'd need to turn that planning over to someone else and bring them up to speed before I could even consider returning."

Luigi drew a deep breath. "Okay. We'll leave it there for now. Get some rest and I'll see you at seven."

On the way to his room, Marc knocked softly on Peg's door. She was expecting him and open the door quickly. She put her finger to her lips and motioned him to follow her to the balcony. "What's going on?" she asked softly.

Marc gave her a run-down on the conversation he'd had with Luigi.

"That's the pits," she said. "He' really fallen for you. Who would have thought?"

"I know," Marc replied. "I like him a lot and I feel like a real shit. I keep thinking that he's a much better person, than you would consider to be second-in-command. Do you suppose he would give it up if he had a choice?"

"Hard to say," Peg said. "I'm not sure he would forgive your deception."

"Yeah, there is that." He replied. "I wonder if Italy has a witness protection program?"

"We could ask Alfredo next time we speak," she responded. "But, asking him to betray his Family is asking a lot. If he were to be threatened with a jail sentence, that might tip the scales."

"I talked to both Alfredo and Peter Just before you came up and filled them in on what happened. Alfredo doesn't have any more thoughts on how to disrupt the arms for cocaine flow. He feels that if we can't stop the operation, we could slow it down and there would be less cocaine be put on the market here in Italy."

"Food for thought," Marc said. "I'll use this quiet time to see what I can come up with. I'll come and get you just before seven."

Peg opened here door and checked to see that the hallway was clear, then Marc walked quietly to his room.

Just before seven, Marc rapped on Peg's door. She joined him as they made their way down the stairs.

"Any new thoughts?" Peg whispered.

"Nope. Maybe we can brain storm something on the plane back to the States." Marc answered.

They entered the great room to find Luigi and Antonio already on their first drink. Scotch for both of you?" asked Luigi. "Yes," the duo answered in chorus.

"Luigi tells me that you'll be leaving tomorrow." Antonio directed to Peg. "I will be sad to see you go."

"Well, it's been a successful trip both business wise and culturally, but it's time to get back and start on plans to expand this operation." She responded.

"That's as close as we will get to talking business until after dinner." Luigi interjected.

The next two hours passed quickly filled mostly with small talk centered around the States. Carlo called them to dinner and they filed into the dining room. When they were seated Luigi announced: "I asked Nicol to prepare something special. This is one of my most favorite dishes. Boar Osso Bucco over polenta. Enjoy."

The Osso Bucco was covered in a heavy brown gravy. There was a side dish of greens beans and the meal was paired with a smooth Chianti. Dessert was vanilla gelato with mixed berries.

"I don't know how you keep in shape with this kind of diet," Peg remarked. "If I ate this way all the time, I'd end up looking like a wine barrel. Again, our complements to Nicol. I didn't think he could top the duck L'Orange, but he certainly did."

Luigi laughed. "I don't eat this way all the time. I just wanted to make your stay as nice as possible. Nicol watches my diet and I work out in the gym regularly. Let's go to the great room for some Armagnac."

When the Armagnac had been poured, Luigi asked: "Is there anything else I can share with you before you return home?"

"No, I think not. There's a lot of planning to do but Maggi and I have been working on an outline. We just need to fill in the blanks when we get home."

Carlo came into the room and cleared his throat. Luigi nodded for him to speak. "Mi scusi signore. C'è una telefonata. So che non ti piace essere disturbato ma hanno detto che era importante." "Excuse me sir. There is a phone call. I know you do not like to be disturbed but they said it was important."

Luigi rose. "Lo prenderò in studio." "I'll take it in the study."

"Lady, gentlemen, excuse me."

The trio sat quietly waiting to learn why Luigi was call away so abruptly. The silence stretched the minutes into making it feel that it was much longer than, in reality, it was just ten minutes. Luigi entered the room with a stern countenance.

"Bad news. Don Giovanni is dead. He was knifed in one of the restrooms at the prison. He normally has his guards with him except in the restroom."

"No!" Exclaimed Antonio. "That's not bad news. That's good news. Now you're the Don."

Luigi glared at Antonio. "That depends on who had him murdered. I might be next. If it was one of the other Families, I don't have much to worry about. If it someone in our Family, then there is going to be a power struggle. It's going to be an interesting time, but I will come out on top! Right now, my bet is on Francisco Ricci. If anything happens to me, he's next in line."

"Antonio, I want you to delay your next trip until we see how this plays out. I need every man to cover my back."

"Luigi, Marc asked. "Is there anything we can do to help?"

"Yes. I'd appreciate it. Can you delay your trip for a few more days?"

"Sure. That' not a problem," Marc responded. What do you want us to do?"

"Right now, help me go through the Villa and insure everything is locked down. Then I want you to get your side arms and stick with me. Antonio, call Alfredo, the driver, and have him head out to the different farms. Have him select one man per farm to come to the Villa to beef up the guards. Then see that all guards have extra magazines. Get three automatic rifles for Maggi, Pietro and myself with extra magazines. Oh, I almost forgot. Get two more weapons and magazines for Nicol and Carlo."

"Si, Don Luigi," Antonio replied.

Luigi stared at Antonio for a moment, shook his head and motioned Peg and Marc to follow him.

There were two wings to the Villa. Luigi directed Marc and Peg each to a wing and took the main house for himself. "Open all the windows and balcony doors and close and lock the wood shutters. Where there are guards on the balconies, leave those doors open. The balconies are too open for the guards to make a stand on them, so they'll need somewhere to fall back to, if the shooting gets heavy. This will not keep someone from breaking in but we should hear them, if they do. Let' meet back in the great room."

Half an hour later, they were all back in the great room.

"You seem to be expecting quite a siege," Peg said.

"Yes I am. The only thing that has stopped Ricci from attacking before was Don Giovanni. He would never accept him as second-in-command. I'm sure Don Giovanni's death was instrumented by Ricci."

"Do you expect him to attack tonight?" Asked Marc.

"No, that's not his style. Unless he's already had his forces mustered, he will be coming tomorrow. Probably late morning. With that in mind, let's all get some rest. The guards will wake us, if I'm wrong."

"Antonio, stay with me for a few minutes. Maggi, Pietro, I'll see you in the morning. Sleep well."

Peg and Marc echoed each other. "Good night."

Luigi followed them to the door way and pulled the heavy doors closed.

"Antonio, ora sei il comandante in seconda, se vuoi il posto." "Antonio, you are now second-in-command, if you want the position."

"Sì, don Luigi. Vorrei la posizione. Grazie." "Yes, Don Luigi. I would like the position. Thank you."

"Con effetto immediato, fermeremo le armi per il commercio di cocaina. Sono sempre stato contrario a portare il traffico di droga nella famiglia. La prossima spedizione in America sarà l'ultima." "Effective immediately, we will stop the arms for cocaine trade. I have always been opposed to bringing drug trade into the Family. This next shipment to America will be the last."

"Ma che dire dei nostri amici americani? Non saranno felici." "But, what about our American friends? They won't be happy."

"Staranno bene. So qualcosa che tu non conosci e che non sono ancora pronto a condividere." "They will be fine. I know something you don't and which I'm not ready to share just yet."

"Riposati. Ci vediamo domani mattina. Buona notte." "Get some rest. I'll see you in the morning. Good night."

"Buona notte don Luigi." "Good night Don Luigi." Antonio left the room, closing the doors softly behind him.

Chapter 28

Villa Falco

Friuli-Venezia Giulia, *Italy*

Next Morning

Marc knocked on Peg's door at seven. She opened the door and joined him in the hallway.

"How did you sleep? He asked.

"Not well," She responded. Leaning close, she whispered: "I don't think our friends at the AISE or for that matter Peter, will be happy that we joined in on a gun battle on Italian soil."

"Well, we could leave it out of our report," Marc chuckled.

They found Luigi and Antonio seated at the dining table having coffee. Breakfast was set out on the side board.

"Eat up," Luigi said. "Lunch may be a little late."

They each filled their plates. Carlo came in and served Peg and Marc coffee. When they finished with the food, Luigi asked Carlo to serve more coffee in the study. When they were settled, Luigi spoke: "I have some news to share with you." Addressing Peg and Marc. "Now that I am the Don, I've decided to stop the arms for cocaine trade." He paused.

Peg and Marc exchanged a surprised look. Then looked back to Luigi.

"I have never wanted to include drug trade into the Family. It's not that financially successfully viable. I'm making much more on the investments I've placed."

"To say the least and I speak for Maggi too. What a surprise! I think our Family will be just as amazed. I'm sure you have given this much thought. We will wait until we return the States to break the news. And, have a fast get-away car waiting at the curb. They will not be happy and will be looking for someone to blame.

"I hope, I've not put you in a bad spot, but I've been thinking about this for a long time."

Carlo came into the room. "Don Luigi. Loro sono qui." "Don Luigi. They are here."

"Well, they are early." Luigi said. "Let's see what we're up against." He led them to a door at the rear of the study. Opening the door and turning on the lights revealing a room with several computers and banks of monitors. The cameras were aimed completely around the villa.

Four black Suburbans were arranged around the villa. One each in front and rear and two at each end of the villa. Each vehicle disgorged six men armed with automatic rifles. They took positions behind the cars. The camera at the front showed a tall man dressed all in black facing the main entrance.

"That's Francisco Ricci," commented Luigi. "He seems to be shouting something." He flipped a switch on the console. The man's voice came through loud and clear.

"Luigi, vieni fuori così possiamo discutere su chi sarà il prossimo Don, come due adulti." "Luigi, come out so we can discuss who will be the next Don, like adults."

"Surely, you are not going out there?" Peg remarked.

"Not likely," Luigi answered. "The man has no honor. We will wait him out to see what he'll do next."

Ricci moved behind the vehicle and shouted: "Fire!" The men at the front started shooting at the villa. The other men around the villa followed suit. Luigi's guards opened fire in response. The rounds quickly shattered the shutters. The front door didn't budge.

"Are your men going to be okay." asked Peg.

"They will be fine," answered Luigi. That's why I directed you to leave the balcony doors open. The just need to step back inside. The bullets won't penetrate the stucco. They began to hear return fire from Luigi's guards. On the monitors, they could see the rounds hitting the vehicles. None of the cars were experiencing any damage.

"Looks like the vehicles are reinforced. Even the windows are not breaking. Seems we'll be here a while. I have an idea. Do you have any sniper rifles?" Marc asked.

"Do you think you can take out Ricci," Luigi asked.

"Not me," Marc replied. "Maggi. She's the marksman."

Peg shrugged her shoulders. "I'll give it a try."

Luigi turned to Antonio. "Get her what she needs."

"I'll be her spotter," Marc added. "I'll need binoculars and a range finder."

Antonio nodded his head and rushed out of the room.

"What's the highest point I can get to in the Villa?" Peg asked.

"There is an attic with small windows on the floor above the bedrooms," Luigi said.

Antonio came into the room with the equipment.

"Antoni, show them how to get up to the attic." Luigi directed.

Peg and Marc followed Antoni out of the room and up the stair case to the second floor. He led them to a door at the end of the hallways. It opened to show a spiral staircase leading up. They found themselves in a dusty room crowded with boxes. The only light came from two small windows.

"I'll open the windows for you," said Antonio.

"Okay," Peg said. "But do it very slowly, so it doesn't draw any attention."

Antonio did as directed.

Marc moved several boxes over to one window to give Peg a purchase for her rifle that allowed her to point down toward the cars. He went to the other window but stayed back so the people below couldn't see him.

Peg looked through her scope and asked: "which one is he?"

"He's the one by the driver's door. No wind. Range fifty yards."

"Got him," she said. "I can only see the top of his head, so this will be a tough shot." She steadied her breathing and pull the trigger.

Ricci's body flew back from the vehicle — the top of his head missing. The men behind that car immediately stopped shooting. Shortly the others stopped too. They piled into the cars and sped away leaving Ricci's body behind.

"Wow! Exclaimed Antonio. "That shot was amazing." The trio closed the windows and went back to the study.

Luigi was waiting for them. Antonio proceeded to babble about the skill Peg exhibited. Addressing both Peg and Marc he said: "Your plan worked. Thank you. The danger is passed."

Peg and Marc grinned. "Guess we can catch our plane tomorrow after all." Peg said.

"I'll be sorry to see you go," Luigi said. "You will be missed."

Marc looked at Peg and got a nod. "Luigi, there's something we need to explain to you."

"I think I know what it is, Margret O'Ryan, Marcus Parker.

There was a stunned silence from everyone in the room. "How…" Marc stuttered.

Luigi laughed. "I have friends in the AISE too."

Chapter 29

CIA Headquarters

Langley, Virginia

Peg and Marc were seated in Peter's office giving a verbal report. They would jointly write one up later. Peter gave his approval. He dismissed them and the duo went to Peg's office.

"What's up Marc? You're very pensive." Asked Peg

"I'm thinking very strongly, that I'm ready to give it up." He replied.

"You mean from the CIA?" She said.

"Yes," he replied. "I enjoy the work and mostly working with you. It's just that I have strong feelings for Luigi and I'd like to explore where that will lead."

"Why don't you take some time off and if things don't work out, you still have a job?"

"No, there's more to it. If I find my soul mate, be it Luigi or someone else, there looms the specter of my being blackmailed if the one I'm with is not out. You know that's something the CIA won't accept."

"So, you are ready to settle down?"

"Yes, definitely."

"What will you do for a living."

"If it's here in the States, probably private security. If Italy, I'll just have to see."

"Boy, this is hard to take," she said.

"I know. I'm sorry. I think, I'd better go see Peter while my courage is still up."

Chapter 30

Villa Falco, Italy

Friuli-Venezia Giulia, *Italy*

A taxi pulled up in front of Villa Falco. Carlo, always on the alert, opened the front door. "Signore Romano, benvenuto. Don Luigi sarà felice di vederti. È stato molto triste da quando te ne sei andato." "Mister Romano, welcome. Don Luigi will be happy to see you. He has been very sad since you left."

"Grazie Carlo, ma è solo Marc Parker. Don Luigi è qui?" "Thank you, Carlo, but it's just Marc Parker. Is Don Luigi here?"

"Si signore. È nello studio. Porterò la tua borsa in camera tua. Conosci la strada per lo studio." "Yes Mister. He is in the study. I will take your bag to your room. You know your way to the study."

Marc mad his way to the study. The door was closed so he knocked.

"Accedere." "Enter." He heard Luigi call out.

Marc open the door and stood in the doorway.

Luigi looked up. Surprise on his face. He stood so abruptly; he knocked his chair over. He rushed to Marc and took him in his arms. "You came back!"

"Is the offer still open," Marc asked.

"Yes, oh yes," Luigi replied and pressed his lips to Marc's.